TESTING TIME

Skye Fargo thought he was the only Anglo on the Otero ranch. But now a new gun was on the payroll.

"As I live and breathe," the Trailsman said sarcastically, "it's Jessie Walker. I should have known you were around. I've been smelling a strange odor."

Walker wasn't alone. He had a crew of fellow killers with him. They started to close in on Fargo.

"No!" Walker bellowed. "This high-and-mighty son of a bitch is mine." He faced Fargo, his hands at waist height. "I've heard a lot about you, Trailsman. They say you're the best. Well, I've got news for you. *I'm* better."

Someone was going to have to swallow his words—and wash them down with blood. . . .

THE
TRAILSMAN
118

ARIZONA
SLAUGHTER

by

Jon Sharpe

A SIGNET BOOK

SIGNET
Published by the Penguin Group
Penguin Books USA Inc., 375 Hudson Street,
New York, New York, 10014, U.S.A.
Penguin Books Ltd, 27 Wrights Lane, London W8 5TZ, England
Penguin Books Australia Ltd, Ringwood, Victoria, Australia
Penguin Books Canada Ltd, 10 Alcorn Avenue, Toronto, Ontario M4V 3B2
Penguin Books (N.Z.) Ltd, 182-190 Wairau Road,
Auckland 10, New Zealand

Penguin Books Ltd, Registered Offices:
Harmondsworth, Middlesex, England

First published by Signet, an imprint of New American Library,
a division of Penguin Books USA Inc.

First Printing, October, 1991

10 9 8 7 6 5 4 3 2 1

Copyright© Jon Sharpe, 1991
All rights reserved

The first chapter of this book originally appeared in *Gun Valley*, the one hundred seventeenth volume in this series.

 REGISTERED TRADEMARK—MARCA REGISTRADA

PRINTED IN THE UNITED STATES OF AMERICA

The Trailsman

Beginnings . . . they bend the tree and they mark the man. Skye Fargo was born when he was eighteen. Terror was his midwife, vengeance his first cry. Killing spawned Skye Fargo, ruthless, cold-blooded murder. Out of the acrid smoke of gunpowder still hanging in the air, he rose, cried out a promise never forgotten.

The Trailsman they began to call him all across the West: searcher, scout, hunter, the man who could see where others only looked, his skills for hire but not his soul, the man who lived each day to the fullest, yet trailed each tomorrow. Skye Fargo, the Trailsman, the seeker who could take the wildness of a land and the wanting of a woman and make them his own.

1859, the Santa Maria Mountains—
a land where Apaches lurked behind every boulder,
wealthy Spaniards lived like kings,
and lone riders usually became buzzard bait . . .

1

The warm wind blowing stiffly from the west carried the sharp crack of the shot for over a mile.

A red hawk circling high over the rugged Santa Maria Mountains heard it and instinctively banked in the opposite direction.

A lone coyote padding up a steep slope heard it and paused to tilt its head and listen.

And a magnificent Ovaro, a black-and-white pinto stallion, heard the sound and pricked up its ears as it moved at a leisurely westward pace along the bank of the shallow Santa Maria River.

The big man astride the Ovaro also listened with interest to the distant shot. As a seasoned frontiersman he easily estimated the distance, then pondered the possibilities, his lake-blue eyes narrowing. It could be a hunter, he reckoned. Or someone out practicing. But since he was miles from any settlement and in the heart of Apache territory, he suspected the shot might have more sinister implications.

Not that he felt any fear. Skye Fargo didn't regard danger as most men did; he relished it. To him, any danger was a challenge to be bested with either his Colt, Sharps rifle, boot knife, or bare knuckles if necessary. He thrived where many a man would cringe, and that was the reason, perhaps more than any other, that men had taken to speaking of him in awed tones around their campfires at night. Never cross the Trailsman, they would say, unless you're looking for a plot of earth six feet under.

Fargo urged the Ovaro into a gallop, his curiosity getting the better of his caution. He must be within ten miles of his destination, the *rancho* of Don Celestino Otero, and it occurred to him that his potential employer might somehow be involved.

The pinto's pounding hooves raised little clouds of dust as the stallion followed the narrow game trail bordering the river up a low rise.

Reining up, Fargo scanned the terrain ahead, a broad expanse of boulder strewn land between two mountains. He saw no one, detected no hint of movement, and clucked the stallion into a gallop again. If he figured it right, the shot had come from the narrow pass between the mountains.

Another shot suddenly confirmed his hunch. Seconds later wholesale firing commenced attended by faint, savage whoops.

There could be no doubt. Apaches were involved. Fargo rode hard toward the pass, the fringe on his buckskins flying in the wind. He threaded a path among the boulders, the stallion responding superbly, the sounds of the conflict growing steadily louder. It sounded like a raging battle was in progress.

The blistering afternoon sun brought beads of sweat to Fargo's brow and he mopped his right sleeve across his forehead. His muscular body flowed smoothly with the motion of his mount, horse and rider as one. Soon he came to a clear tract. Beyond was a jumble of boulders, then the pass.

As Fargo crossed the level ground, his mind flashed back to the reason for his presence in these remote mountains few white men had ever seen. A week ago he had arrived in Tucson, tired and saddle sore, after leading a small wagon train all the way from Missouri. He'd looked forward to a few days of rest and relaxation and then he would be back on the trail, heading north into the Rockies. But it wasn't in the cards.

On the third morning of his Tucson stay, a Spaniard had shown up at his hotel door and requested to speak with him. The man, one Jose Rojos, presented himself as the foreman for a wealthy rancher named Celestino Otero. For some time a band of fierce Apaches had been harassing Otero mercilessly, and unless something was done soon the vast *rancho* would be ruined. Otero had sent his foreman to Tucson in the hope of securing the services of men willing to fight the dreaded Apaches on their own terms. There had been no takers, and Rojos was all set to leave and break the bad news to his *patron* when he heard Fargo was in town.

A grim smile touched Fargo's lips at the memory. If he possessed a shred of common sense he would have declined the offer. But the promise of a gold *peso* for every day he stayed on the job and the sheer challenge of it were too tempting to resist.

Preoccupied with his thoughts, Fargo didn't see the other rider until he was almost to the boulders. Suddenly an Indian burst into view. Fargo hauled on the reins, his right hand sweeping to the Colt, and he had the revolver leveled, his thumb beginning to pull the hammer back, when he realized he'd be shooting an unarmed man.

Swaying precariously on a fine brown stallion, his head bowed and his chin touching his chest, an Apache warrior came straight toward the Trailsman. His arms dangled uselessly at his sides; if not for the pressure of his legs on the animal he would surely have fallen. Except for a leather loincloth and high moccasins, the sinewy warrior was naked, his skin bronzed by constant exposure to the sun, his long hair bound at the forehead with a strip of deer skin. The horse he rode drew up of its own accord within ten feet of the Ovaro.

Fargo slowly lowered the Colt. He saw a neat hole high on the left side of the warrior's chest. Blood flowed steadily from the wound, which might well prove fatal.

Unexpectedly the Apache looked up, his pain-filled eyes resting on the big man and taking Fargo's measure. The warrior's weathered features betrayed no hostility. He stared for all of ten seconds, then his eyelids fluttered and his chin sagged again.

The shooting in the pass had died off.

Holstering the Colt, Fargo moved closer to the stallion, noting the fine Spanish bridle and saddle its previous owner must have valued very highly. He went to reach for the drooping reins when more gunfire erupted ahead, punctuated by a sound that galvanized him into instant action—the high, piercing shriek of a terrified woman.

Once more the pinto displayed its wing-footed speed. Fargo craned his neck for a glimpse of the gap between the towering peaks. He came within a dozen yards of his destination and spied a fancy Spanish-style wagon overturned. Nearby were prone figures. Before he could identify them he rode past a high boulder and a shadow swooped down from above.

A heavy body slammed into the big man's shoulders and sent him flying from the pinto. Fargo came down hard on his right side, rolling to the right at the moment of impact and clawing for his Colt. He rose to his knee at the same moment his attacker plowed into him again, knocking him onto his back.

An Apache was on his chest and lifting a knife for the death stroke.

Fargo reacted instinctively, his right fist crunching into the warrior's mouth, his left clamping on the man's knife arm. He rolled and heaved, flinging the dazed Apache from him, then rose, the Colt clearing leather as he uncoiled.

Undaunted, the Apache blinked once and charged again.

Magnified by the boulders, the blast of the Colt seemed to echo and reecho. The ball caught the warrior in the center of his forehead and flipped him backward to lie still in the dirt. A small cloud of acrid gunsmoke hung in the air between them.

There was no time or need for Fargo to check the body. Whirling, he ran to where the pinto had stopped almost at the edge of the pass, worried an Apache might reach his mount before he did. Sure enough, a lean warrior dashed from out of nowhere, a tomahawk in hand, and raced toward the Ovaro. Fargo shot the man on the run, hitting him in the left temple. In an ungainly swirl of limbs the Apache toppled.

Mayhem prevailed in the pass. Apaches and *vaqueros* were engaged in a furious fight with half a dozen corpses from each side littering the ground. The Indians had taken cover in rocks on the south side while the *vaqueros* were in similar cover to the north. Rifles and pistols boomed. Arrows and a few lances streaked across the gap.

All of this Fargo took in as he grabbed the pinto's reins and pulled the horse into the welcome shelter of a boulder. He peered out again, taking stock, seeking targets to shoot. As near as he could tell the Apaches had ambushed a party of *vaqueros* on their way to the *rancho*. Apparently the gruesome stories of Apache atrocities related by Jose Rojos were true.

He saw a number of dead and wounded horses in the pass and frowned, hearing their frightened whinnies and wishing he could put them out of their misery. To his way of thinking, hurting a poor horse amounted to callous cruelty. He'd never met a horse he didn't like, which was more than he could say about most men.

A commotion in the rocks to the south arrested Fargo's attention. Two warriors were in the process of hauling a woman of distinctly Spanish origin, who was kicking and clawing furiously, to the southwest. They evidently planned to spirit her back to their village.

The *vaqueros* on the north side of the pass realized her plight and mounted a concerted rescue attempt. Over a dozen men, all in wide-brimmed hats and leather chaps, sprinted toward the Indians, firing hastily and shouting curses at their enemies. Their valiant attempt proved futile as four of them were struck by arrows before they had gone a third of the way. The rest paused, their nerve shattered, still shooting wildly. Yet another *vaquero* died, screaming with a shaft through his chest, and the remainder broke for the north side and shelter.

Fargo watched the two warriors move farther away. The other Apaches were loosing more arrows to deter pursuit. Nodding, he swung into the saddle and headed to the southwest, using every available boulder to screen him from hostile eyes. If he moved paralleled to the base of the mountain for a spell, he should be able to intercept the two Apaches and their captive out of sight of the rest of the band.

He hunched low over the pommel, glancing up at the side of the slope, occasionally spotting the threesome. The woman struggled tirelessly and he found himself admiring her courage. Abruptly, twenty yards later, he lost sight of them.

Stopping, Fargo probed the rocks and scraggly brush, concerned they would elude him. Where the hell could they have gone? Moments later they reappeared, only all three were on horses. They raced to the south, angling down the mountain. Perfect, he reflected, grinning, and moved to cut them off at the base. The warriors were engrossed in keeping the woman between them while negotiating a narrow trail and had no inkling of his presence.

Fargo slanted toward them, going from cover to cover. Gunshots and yells indicated that the fight still raged in the pass. He came to a barren knoll that concealed him from the descending pair of Apaches, reined sharply to the right, and mentally ticked off a count of ten. Then, with his lips curled grimly and the Colt cocked in his right hand, he galloped up and over the knoll, intending to catch the warriors by surprise.

Instead, his own eyes widened at finding *another* pair of Apaches waiting thirty feet away at the bottom of the mountain for their companions, who along with the woman had another dozen yards to go. Both men spun their mounts at the sound of the pinto's arrival on the scene. Both voiced defiant cries and charged.

Talk about bad luck. Fargo had no choice but to meet them head-on. There was nowhere to take cover and running away never entered his head. He bore down on the two warriors at a full gallop. The Indian on the right carried a lance, the one on the left a bow. He shot the bowman first as the warrior was pulling the string back and barely glimpsed the man toppling to the earth as he shifted his aim to the second Apache and squeezed off another shot.

The Apache reeled but stayed on his animal. He lifted the slender spear on high. At a range of fifteen feet he couldn't miss, even though wounded.

Fargo thumbed off two quick blasts, the rolling motion of the Ovaro throwing his aim off a mite but both struck the onrushing warrior in the head and catapulted the Apache off his horse.

By this time the woman and her captors had reached the base of the mountain. One already had a shaft nocked in a stout bow, which he now let fly.

Fargo saw the archer fire and instantly swung low on the left side of the pinto, holding on with his right forearm looped around the pommel and his right leg draped over the stallion's back. The arrow flashed past overhead, narrowly missing the Ovaro. Had he still been sitting in the saddle the shaft would have entered his chest.

He hauled himself up and holstered the empty Colt while coming to a stop, then whipped the Sharps from its saddle holster. Levering a round into the chamber he took deliberate aim, and a heartbeat before the Indian loosed another deadly shaft, he fired. The big rifle boomed, bucking against his shoulder, and the warrior fell, the arrow sailing into the nearby ground.

Fargo scanned the mountain and saw no other Apaches. The woman, a raven-haired beauty who appeared to be in her early twenties, regarded him in astonishment. He rode over to her and bestowed a friendly smile. "Hello, ma'am. *Buenas tardes, senorita*. The name is Skye Fargo. I strongly suggest we leave here while we can."

Up close her soft features were incredibly lovely, her complexion flawless. Frank brown eyes regarded him with a mixture of curiosity and fear. Her brown blouse and long black skirt, both soiled with dirt, clung suggestively to her shapely figure. The blouse had been ripped in her struggle and partially exposed the swelling top of her left breast.

"Didn't you hear me, lady?" Fargo reiterated. "*Habla ingles*? We've got to get out of here before more Apaches come." He moved a bit nearer, intending to lay a hand on her shoulder to snap her out of her daze.

Without warning the tigress cupped her hands together and swept her arms in a vicious arc.

Taken unawares, Fargo was hit on the chin. The blow rocked him in the saddle, jamming his teeth together and making him see bright pinpoints of swirling light. The pinto shied and he tugged on the reins, getting the animal under control. When next he glanced at the woman she was heading to the southwest at top speed. "Dammit," he groused under his breath, and took off in pursuit. For all he knew, she might blunder into another band of Apaches. He had to save her in spite of herself.

2

The Spanish tigress rode with the skill of someone who had been weaned on horseback, her long hair flowing behind her. She glanced back repeatedly, her fury obvious at seeing the big man rapidly narrow the gap. The closer he came, the more she whipped her mount with the reins.

Fargo shoved the Sharps into its holster and concentrated on avoiding rocks and animal burrows. He couldn't wait to get his hands on her again. The panic that came over her features as he overtook her almost compensated for the blow to the chin. Almost, but not quite.

He came alongside her mount. She ceased flogging her horse and began flailing away at him, attempting to lash his eyes with the ends of the length of rope constituting the war bridle. Jerking his head back, he avoided her frantic swings. Then, when her arm momentarily drooped, he edged the pinto in next to her horse, leaned down, and scooped her into his left arm.

Predictably the woman fought him as if she thought her life was in danger, pounding his arm and kicking the stallion's sides. "Let go of me, *gringo!*" she screeched indignantly.

Why not? Skye thought, spying a small mesquite directly ahead. He was strongly tempted to dump her on it, but the image of what the sharp thorns would do to her tender flesh dissuaded him. Instead, he slowed, skirted the mesquite, and let go.

With an inarticulate cry the woman tumbled onto the dirt, winding up on her posterior and glaring at him with her fists balled.

Fargo made a tight circle and returned to her side, his mocking grin only seeming to antagonize her further. "Are you done behaving like a damned fool?"

"*Gringo* pig!" she spat, her rosy lips forming a delicious oval.

He leaned on the saddle horn and smirked. "I know if *I* was

16

stranded in the middle of Apache country, I'd be a bit more polite to someone who could give me a ride."

"I had a ride, *bastardo,*" she snapped, rising and swiping at the dust on her clothes.

Fargo twisted and saw her mount racing to the southwest. "I reckon if you run real fast you might catch him by next year."

"You son of a bitch," the tigress declared. Turning, she started to walk due east.

"And where do you figure you're going?"

"It is none of your business."

Sighing, Fargo trailed after her. "Mind telling me your name?"

"Go to hell."

"Is this the thanks I get for saving your hide from those Chiricahua Apaches?" Fargo asked testily.

The question caused her to pause and squint up at him. "You know which tribe they are from? Interesting. I didn't think most Anglos could tell them apart." She resumed walking, her shoulders squared, her slender back arched, her breasts jutting against her blouse.

Fargo looked behind him, then gazed at the expanse of arid land ahead. "There could be more Apaches out there right now looking at us."

She drew up short and apprehensively surveyed the horizon. "I don't see any. You're just trying to frighten me."

"Think what you want. But I don't aim to stick around much longer. Are you coming with me or not?"

The woman halted and faced him. "Will you let me ride your pinto?"

Fargo indicated the back of his stallion with a jerk of his thumb. "Climb on board."

"I would rather sit on a prickly pear than ride with you," she stated.

Shrugging, Fargo slowly swung the pinto around. "Fine, lady. You and your pride can shrivel in this sun while I ride back to that pass." He began to make good on his bluff when she called out.

"Wait, *hombre.* I have no choice. I will go with you."

Stopping, Fargo locked his steely eyes on hers. "The name

is Skye Fargo," he reminded her. "Not *gringo*, not *hombre*, not pig. Understand?"

"*Si,*" she replied rather meekly, and ran to the Ovaro. "I will be very grateful if you will take me with you to the pass. The *vaqueros* will take care of my needs from there."

"If they're still alive," Fargo said, extending his right hand.

She hesitated, then took hold of his arm and let herself be swung effortlessly up behind him.

"Hold on to my waist," Fargo cautioned.

"I am fine, thanks."

Shaking his head at her stubbornness, Fargo headed to the east. At the first lurching rhythm of the big horse his passenger quickly draped her arms around his midsection and held on tight. He could feel her soft bosom pressing against his back and had a hard time keeping his mind on the matter at hand.

"My name, *senor,*" she unexpectedly volunteered, "is Gitana Otero."

The daughter of the top man himself. Fargo was mildly surprised that the rancher would let his daughter roam the countryside with Apaches on the warpath. "Doesn't your father own a spread hereabouts?"

"It is not a spread," Gitana said, accenting the last word distastefully. "The Otero *hacienda* is the grandest north of Mexico City."

"Your father raises more than stock, does he?"

"*Si.* Half of our valley is cultivated for the growing of crops. There are many mouths to feed, what with all the hands we have."

"And how many would that be?"

"Sixty-three counting the house servants and the laborers who till our fields," Gitana answered, using a tone that implied she regarded both classes in a less than flattering light.

Fargo, alert for an ambush, mulled over her answers. He'd only known her a short while, but already he pegged her as a spoiled aristocrat who tended to put on airs around her presumed inferiors. The combination of beauty and excessive pride marked her as potential trouble.

They rode ever closer to the spot where he'd slain the Apaches. He took the opportunity to reload the Colt, carefully

18

sliding the cartridges into the chambers, then placing the caps on the nipples behind each cartridge. His .44 could fire either the ball type of cartridge or the newer conical bullet variety. He'd been using the bullets ever since they first came out. They shot straight and true and could down a man at forty yards. While in Tucson he'd purchased dozens to see him through until the next time he visited civilization.

The shooting at the pass had died down, whether because one side or the other had triumphed or the battle had simply ended in a draw there was no way of telling.

"What are you doing in this territory, *senor*?" Gitana asked.

"A man named Rojos hired me to lend your father a hand in dealing with the Apaches."

For several seconds Gitana made no response. Then she said, rather contritely, "I had no idea. My father can use all the help he can get, particularly from a brave man such as yourself. Please forgive my bad manners earlier."

Fargo merely nodded, amused by her abrupt turnaround. One minute she regarded him as a bastard; now that she knew he intended to assist her pa, she was all honey and cream.

"And I haven't properly thanked you for saving my life," Gitana added. "If those savages had taken me off to their filthy village, the strain of worrying about me would have killed my poor father. The doctor has told him that his heart may well give out under too much stress."

"Your father is ailing?"

"*Si*. He suffered great chest pains over a year ago and hasn't been the same man since. It is a good thing my mother is not alive to see how much he has changed," Gitana said. Then she went on bitterly, "My mother was killed by Apaches three years ago. They butchered her after first violating her womanhood."

Odd, Fargo thought. Apaches rarely raped woman captives. They preferred to adopt females into the tribe to bear their young. The Chiricahuas giving Otero so much trouble must be a particularly vicious band.

As if on cue, a large band of Indians abruptly appeared, riding out from behind the mountain and making to the southeast.

Fargo instantly wheeled the pinto behind a boulder the size of a cabin and peeked out to mark the progress of the Apaches.

Several of them, evidently wounded, were being assisted by other warriors. He tried counting them but the cloud of dust they raised made the task impossible.

"My *vaqueros* have sent them running," Gitana declared spitefully. "The next time we will wipe them out."

Waiting until the last of the Indians disappeared from view, Fargo moved from concealment. He'd only gone a dozen yards when another group of riders materialized.

"The *vaqueros*!" Gitana cried.

Before Fargo could say a word, she began shouting at the top of her lungs in Spanish. One of the lead riders, a man in black wearing a flat-topped hat with a broad brim, heard her yell and reined up. Soon all nine of the men were hastening to their mistress.

Unexpectedly, Gitana Otero dropped to the ground and walked forward a yard to stand beaming with her hands on her attractive hips.

Fargo rested his right hand near his holster. These *vaqueros* were supposed to be his allies, but he'd learned a long time ago never to take anything or anyone for granted. A person lived longer that way.

Most of the *vaqueros*, who were simple cowhands, wore expressions of bewilderment. A few regarded the Trailsman suspiciously. Foremost among them was the man in black, who wore a black leather holster inlaid with silver and whose Dragoon sported pearl grips.

Gitana addressed them, motioning several times at her rescuer. The man in black did all the talking for the *vaqueros*. From his manner and the cold glances he bestowed on Fargo, it became apparent he was displeased at the turn of events. At last Gitana turned and smiled.

"You are welcome to ride back to the *hacienda* with us, Senor Fargo."

"Call me Skye," Fargo said, not bothering to mention that he'd comprehended the gist of their conversation. He spoke enough Spanish to know that Gitana had gloated over all the Apaches slain and that the head *vaquero* keenly resented his presence. For now he'd let the matter go.

"Very well, Skye. I am most anxious for you to meet my father. We will leave immediately."

The man in black barked orders to a skinny *vaquero,* who promptly dismounted and climbed up behind another man.

Gitana walked to his horse and swung up into the saddle. She motioned for Fargo to ride beside her, and at the head of her men they returned to the pass. No one bothered to speak until they arrived.

Bodies dotted both slopes as well as the ground near the overturned wagon—actually a coach more suited to city use than the rugged mountainous terrain. A *vaquero* lying on his back, his chest transfixed by two arrows, was twitching feebly. Otherwise, none of the bodies displayed any trace of life.

"If you don't mind, Skye," Gitana said, "we will take the time to bury our dead. The coach must stay where it is since the team ran off when it went down. I'll send more men back for it later, but I'm afraid the savages will destroy it before then. What a shame. My father had it brought all the way from Santa Fe."

Fargo gazed idly at the conveyance. Was it his imagination, or did she seem more concerned about the loss of the coach than the loss of those *vaqueros* who had died protecting her?

While the rest of the men tended to scooping shallow graves for their fallen *compadres,* the man in black went to the coach and rummaged inside until he found what he wanted: a woman's riding jacket that he promptly brought over to Gitana. She thanked him and donned it to cover her ripped blouse.

Fargo moved near a cluster of low boulders and climbed down. He rested on one of the boulders while watching the graves being dug. In the back of his mind he was troubled, but he couldn't put his finger on the exact reason. Certain aspects of the Apache attack just didn't add up. For one thing, it wasn't like Apaches to give up so easily. There had been more Apaches left than *vaqueros,* and under normal circumstances the warriors would have fought on until every *vaquero* was dead. Then, too, if the Apaches had sprung an ambush on the *vaqueros,* very few of the herdsmen would have survived the first few swarms of arrows. It didn't make sense and he resolved to get to the bottom of the mystery as soon as he could.

Gitana strolled over, her hands clasped behind her back. She leaned on a boulder and eyed him critically. "Have you killed many men, Skye Fargo?"

The blunt question took Fargo offguard. He blinked and hesitated before responding. "My share, I reckon. Why?"

"You were superb against those savages. I'd say you're almost as good as Feliz," Gitana said, nodding at the man in black who was busy overseeing the digging. "He is a very deadly man, *senor,* and I would not cross him if I were you. They say he has killed a man for every year of his life."

Fargo guessed the man in black to be in his thirties.

"Reyes Feliz isn't a man to be trifled with," Gitana emphasized.

"I'll keep it in mind," Fargo said dryly. Why was she making such a big issue of it? He wasn't looking for a fight, but he wouldn't avoid one, either.

Gitana made a show of brushing at her hair and moving the top of her blouse back and forth to fan her chest. "I must look a sight. When we get back, the first thing I will do is take a long, hot bath."

Imagining what she would look like naked and covered with suds, Fargo started to smirk. That was when he detected movement out of the corner of his eye and looked up at the slope of the mountain to the south to behold a wounded Apache in the act of pulling back the string on a bow. The warrior's arrow was aimed directly at Gitana.

3

Fargo's right hand swooped to his Colt, but as fast as he was, someone else had already spied the Apache and beaten him to the draw.

Reyes Feliz cleared leather in a blur and extended his Dragoon. He rushed his shot, missing by a hair, striking a rock near the warrior.

Undaunted, the Apache released the shaft anyway and dived from sight.

As if in slow motion, Fargo followed the flight of the streaking arrow and instinctively realized it would be right on target. He sprang into motion, lunging at Gitana and curling his arms around her soft abdomen, hearing her squeal in surprise as he pulled her down on top of him. He landed on his back, her supple form flush with his own. For a moment her face was close to his, their noses almost touching, her warm breath on his mouth.

Gunfire broke out right and left around them.

"Are you all right, ma'am?" Fargo inquired ever-so-politely, savoring the pliant feel of her body on his.

Gitana glanced at the wildly firing *vaqueros*, then turned into the Trailsman's eyes. "Why did you do that?" she demanded indignantly, but not *too* indignantly.

Noticing that she made no move to get off him, Fargo brazenly let his hands rest on her hips. He wasn't concerned about the lone Apache; the *vaqueros* would keep the warrior pinned down. "I saved your life," he informed her.

"Oh?"

Fargo twisted his head and saw the shaft partially imbedded in the ground a few yards past the boulder she'd been leaning on. He nodded toward it. "See for yourself."

Shifting, unconsciously rubbing her body against his, Gitana saw the arrow. She maintained her composure and said simply,

23

"Gracias." Then she put her palms on his shoulders and shoved upright.

Fargo rose and faced to the south. Feliz and other *vaqueros* had fanned out into the rocks and were searching for the Apache. He was surprised when they found him, as attested to by their shouts and whoops of joy. The warrior must be badly wounded or they would never have taken the man alive.

Feliz led the procession of exultant herdsmen and their captive down to the pass. The *vaqueros* surrounded the Indian, a warrior in his forties whose left shoulder and midsection were covered with blood, and the man in black began questioning the Apache in Spanish.

Gitana hurried over.

The hatred reflected in the features of the *vaqueros* left little doubt as to the impending fate of the warrior. Fargo scowled. When it came time for him to cash in his chips, he hoped to hell he wasn't in the same situation. Being unarmed, defenseless, and at the mercy of one's enemies had to rank as just about the worst way possible to die. He'd rather go out with his guns blazing and never see the bullet with his name on it.

Gitana began questioning the prisoner herself. She became increasingly infuriated by the warrior's failure to respond. At length she spoke softly to Feliz.

The man in black abruptly slapped the Apache across the mouth. When the warrior staggered and would have fallen, a pair of *vaqueros* came forward and seized him by the arms to keep him on his feet.

Again Gitana posed questions. Again the Apache remained tightlipped.

Feliz waded into the Indian with his fists flying, landing brutal blow after brutal blow to the warrior's chest and stomach. Grimacing and clearly in acute pain, the Apache never cried out or begged for mercy.

The warrior's stoic endurance made an eloquent appeal to Fargo's sense of fair play. If they were going to kill the Apache, they should do the deed and get it over with, not indulge in sadistic torture. No one paid any attention to him as he ambled over to the line of *vaqueros* and stood with his right thumb hooked in his gunbelt, his hand within inches of the Colt. He observed Feliz pounding away, saw the twisted grin on Gitana's face, and felt a flicker of indignation.

The man in black smashed a fist into the Apache's mouth, then drew back his left arm for another blow.

"That's enough," Fargo barked.

All eyes swung toward the big man.

"Don't interfere," Gitana said. "This doesn't concern you." She pointed at the Apache. "This savage must know the current location of their village and we'll take whatever steps are necessary to get the information from him."

"How can he tell you anything if he doesn't speak Spanish?"

"How do you know he doesn't?" Gitana rejoined. "Even if he can't, we'll get our point across one way or another."

"Not by beating him to death."

"I said this doesn't concern you."

"I came here to hire on with your father, didn't I? Everything you do concerns me," Fargo commented, his hand easing a couple of inches closer to his .44. "Besides, I can find their village for you."

"Our men have tried many times over the years without success," Gitana said. "Are you that much better than them?"

"I'm one of the best there is at what I do," Fargo stated matter-of-factly. "And I know Indians inside and out. I've lived with them, hunted them, and killed them when necessary, but I've never killed one who couldn't fight back." He stared at Feliz. "Only a coward beats a helpless man."

Reyes Feliz abruptly spun, his hand hovering near his Dragoon. "Are you calling *me* a coward, Anglo?" he demanded in near-perfect English.

Not letting his surprise show, Fargo answered in a flinty tone. "What if I am?"

Bloodshed seemed imminent until Gitana stepped between them and glared at them. "That's enough from both of you! I won't have our best men quarreling among themselves. We're on the same side. It's us against the Chiricahuas."

Feliz clenched and unclenched his right hand, the left corner of his mouth jerking up and down. He glowered, then snapped, "As you wish, my lady. If the softhearted *gringo* does not want this poor Apache to be hurt, then we will put the *bastardo* out of his misery.''

Fargo sensed what would occur a hair before it happened, but there was nothing he could do to prevent it. He saw Feliz pivot, saw the Dragoon leap clear, and heard the booming retort as the man in black put a slug into the top of the warrior's head. Blood and brains spattered onto some of the nearby *vaqueros*, then the Apache slumped and the pair holding him let him fall.

With a flourish, Feliz twirled the Dragoon into its holster and smirked at Fargo. ''Are you happy?''

''I am,'' Gitana replied quickly. ''Now let's finish burying our people and head for the *hacienda*. I would like to get home before supper.''

Fargo turned and stalked to the pinto. Eventually he would have a showdown with Reyes Feliz; he just knew it. If that man was a typical *vaquero*, then Fargo was the Queen of England. He'd seen Feliz's type before, *pistoleros* who would go on the prod at the drop of a hat. Their specialty was killing, plain and simple. And usually their services could be purchased for the right price.

''Skye?''

''What do you want?'' Fargo responded without bothering to turn around. A hand fell gently on his broad shoulder and he looked back at Gitana Otero. Her anger evaporated and she smiled.

''Please forgive Feliz. He forgets his station sometimes. But he has been very effective in helping us deal with our Indian problem.''

''How did all of this start?''

''I'll tell you on the ride back,'' Gitana promised, and went off to issue instructions to her men.

It took all of fifteen minutes for the burying to be done with. The *vaqueros* mounted up, Feliz at their head. Gitana Otero took the lead, and with the Trailsman at her side they rode west along the pass. Once past the mountains the vista broadened out into an incredible sight.

Nestled in an immense natural basin formed by a protective ring of outer mountains was a verdant valley with grass and trees. Several streams, meandering down from the high elevations, afforded ample water to cultivate the soil and keep the range covered with lush grass for the grazing of countless cattle.

From the rim of the pass Fargo could see thousands of cows. He also spied small herds of horses. Toward the center of the valley, in the midst of tall trees, was the *hacienda* proper, consisting of a huge white house and numerous other buildings. Immediately surrounding the structures were acres of tilled land devoted to corn, grains, and vegetables.

Gitana, a devilish twinkle in her eyes, glanced at the big man and asked, "Are you impressed?"

"I had no idea," Fargo admitted. Here lay a veritable oasis in the middle of the Santa Maria Mountains. No wonder the Apaches wanted the Otero family driven out. Such a natural paradise would enable the Indians to thrive.

They descended a winding trail into the valley. There, a narrow road, little more than a flattened track, led toward the house. A number of *vaqueros* were tending the stock, and most waved and called out greetings to the returning party.

As promised, Gitana launched into a detailed account of the Otero family history. She appeared to answer Fargo's infrequent questions honestly. Her pride in her family's accomplishments and her determination to keep the land at all costs came through loud and clear.

Fargo listened attentively. The history of the Otero clan dovetailed with the history of the region in general and there were no surprises until near the end of her recital.

Celestino Otero's great-grandfather, a wealthy, adventurous Spaniard whose parents had moved from Spain to the New World in 1710, discovered the valley in 1753 while serving as an officer in the Spanish army. On a routine patrol out of the fort at Tubac, the great-grandfather had recognized the valley's potential right away and, upon his discharge, had packed up all his possessions, taken his retainers, and with a military escort had moved from his estate in Sonora.

The great-grandfather later took a bride. The *hacienda* was constructed. By supplying quality beef and horses to the Spanish army, the Oteros prospered.

All went well until Mexico won its independence from Spain in 1821. Because the Oteros had supplied animals to those in power, the newly formed Mexican government saw fit to cancel all contracts. Celestino Otero, then a young man of twenty, had traveled to Mexico City and persuaded the new rulers to change their minds. Soon the Oteros were back in business, reaping high profits, safe and snug in their tiny domain.

Then, in 1846, the United States went to war with Mexico. The U.S. took control of the region. Suddenly the Oteros were deprived of their sole source of income since they were no longer permitted to supply stock to Mexico. So they had switched and were now selling their cattle to buyers in Santa Fe and Tuscon.

"The money is not so important any more," Gitana concluded as they drew close to the tilled fields. "We have more wealth than we will ever need. But we do have the *vaqueros*, our farm hands, and our servants to think about. They rely on us for their livelihoods."

"When did the Apaches first appear?" Fargo asked, surveying the neatly tilled rows of corn. There were over a dozen men and women at work picking weeds, hoeing, and watering.

"Oh, about four years ago. The Mexican *federales* drove them out of Mexico and they came into this area. They started by stealing our cattle and horses. Then they began conducting raids on the *hacienda*. We have tried everything to drive them off but they're most persistent."

"No one has ever branded Apaches as quitters," Fargo remarked.

"These are devils. They have killed fourteen *vaqueros* and six of our field hands in the past year. Obtaining replacements has proven very difficult. I fear if things continue in this vein, our help will desert us and my father and I will be forced to abandon our home."

"Have you tried asking the government for help?"

"*Si.* But there are too few troops in this region and none can be spared to maintain a constant watch over our precious valley. Every so often a patrol will pay us a visit. During such times the Apaches leave us alone. They're very clever."

Fargo pondered her disclosure. It was odd that the Chiricahuas or one of the other Apache tribes living in the territory hadn't stumbled on the valley ages ago. In fact, it struck him as damned peculiar. Indians always became intimately familiar with the area in which they lived. For the Apaches not to know about

28

such a lush valley was virtually impossible. "Maybe you should set up a palavar between the Apache leader and your father."

"Never," Gitana said emphatically.

"What could it hurt? If you give them a corner of the valley to live in, they might leave you in peace," Fargo pointed out.

"Strike a deal with those savages?" Gitana laughed at the notion. "I would sooner shoot myself."

Fargo added bloodthirsty to the female firebrand's growing list of charater traits. He stared thoughtfully at the house they were approaching. His earlier premonition of something being wrong, of things not quite adding up the way they should, returned, only stronger. It gave him an itchy feeling between his shoulder blades, as if someone was pointing a gun at his back and was only waiting for the right moment to pull the trigger.

4

To say that the Otero *hacienda* was magnificent would be a great understatement. Constructed in the grand Spanish style, the huge house could have graced the street of any wealthy district in Madrid and never raised an eyebrow. In addition to the house there was a barn, a separate stable for the better horses, a building for scores of chickens, quarters for the servants, and a two-tiered bunkhouse for the *vaqueros*. A meticulously maintained lawn contained several flower gardens.

Gitana dismissed all of the *vaqueros* except Reyes Feliz, who accompanied the Trailsman and her to the house. There, a manservant of Mexican lineage took their mounts. Fargo grabbed his rifle and saddlebags before dismounting and walking up the front steps. Feliz opened the door and stood aside so his mistress and Fargo could enter.

Coming down a wide stairway from the second floor was an elderly Spanish gentleman dressed in an immaculate Spanish-stye suit. Both his neatly cropped hair and mustache were grey. His lined features broke into a broad grin as he laid his eyes on Gitana and he called out heartily in Spanish.

Fargo stood with hat in hand while the elderly Spaniard and Gitana embraced and exchanged pleasantries. He assumed the man was her father and she soon confirmed it by introducing them.

"Skye, this is my *padre*. Regrettably, he doesn't speak fluent English. He hired a tutor to teach both of us the language after the United States took control of this region, but he never had the time to stick with his lessons. I've told him a little about you and he is very pleased to make your acquaintance."

Celestino Otero nodded and offered his hand.

"Tell him I'm looking forward to helping him out of the fix he's in," Fargo said, shaking and noting that the Spaniard's grip was weak, his complexion pale. There could be no doubt Celestino was a sickly man.

Gitana translated, listened to her father's response, and smiled at Fargo. "He says he will reward you handsomely if you can drive the Apaches off. He wants to go to his grave knowing I can live on in our valley in peace." She turned to Celestino and spoke at length.

Fargo became aware of Feliz staring at him and returned the favor until the *pistolero* averted his gaze.

"My father has consented to my request to have you stay in our humble house," Gitana said happily. "Would such an arrangement be agreeable to you?"

"Sleep here?" Fargo said, looking in awe at the ornate furnishings. He wasn't accustomed to such elegant lodgings. Give him a blanket and the stars overhead any time. But then he glanced at Gitana, at the expectant gleam in her eyes, at her luscious figure, and decided that a man shouldn't let himself get into a rut. A little novelty now and then never hurt anyone. "Sure. Why not?"

"Excellent. I will show you to your room and you can wash up before supper."

Feliz abruptly cleared his throat and addressed Gitana in Spanish. She replied curtly. Giving a slight bow, he wheeled and departed.

Celestino spoke to his daughter, who looked at the Trailsman.

"My father wants to know why Jose Rojos didn't return with you from Tucson?"

"Your foreman told me that he planned to stay on another week or so to try and recruit a few more men," Fargo explained. "He figured finding me was a good omen and would change his string of luck."

Gitana relayed the news, then motioned for Skye to follow her. "This way, please."

Nodding at her father, Fargo dutifully trailed her up the stairway to a wide corridor and along it to a white door that she threw wide open. He entered a plush bedroom furnished in expensive good taste. "I'm surprised your *padre* would agree to letting a stranger sleep in your house," he commented, stepping to a corner and depositing the Sharps and saddlebags.

"The Otero family is noted for its hospitality," Gitana said,

31

and added with a grin, "Then, too, I asked him to do it."

"And he always does whatever you want?"

"Always."

Add spoiled to the list, Fargo reflected, stepping to a double bed sporting the cleanest white quilt he'd ever laid eyes on. He leaned down and touched it, amazed at its softness, then straightened and turned. And nearly collided with Gitana Otero, who stood inches away with her hands behind her back and a mischievous grin on her lovely face.

"Do you like it?"

"I think I'll get a good night's sleep," Fargo said dryly, letting his eyes rove over her soft neck and down lower.

"You have the look of a wolf about you," Gitana said. "A very handsome wolf."

"Wolves can be dangerous," Fargo noted, dropping his hat on the bed. He couldn't quite figure her out. Was she playing some sort of game? Just a few hours ago she'd called him every dirty name she could think of, ladylike of course. Now she wanted him to spend the night. Maybe he should add fickle to the list also.

"How dangerous?" Gitana asked, posing the question as a challenge. She lowered her arms, her expression inviting.

To hell with it, Fargo thought. Now wasn't the right time to be trying to understand her. He swept her into her arms and planted a hard kiss on her soft lips, feeling them part and her tongue flick out to touch his own. His brawny hands roamed over her back and down onto her behind.

Gitana made a cooing sound deep in her throat.

Fargo slowly brought his hands around her thighs, caressing her legs through her skirt. He rubbed upward until his right hand pressed on the mound at the junction of her legs and she melted against him, her arms coming up around his neck. His right strayed higher until his fingers cupped her left breast. He squeezed, her attendant groan arousing fire in his loins.

Suddenly Gitana broke the kiss and pushed back, her face flushed with passion, her breasts heaving. "*Madre de dios,*" she breathed, and gulped. She seemed shocked by her reaction to his kiss.

He pulled her back to him.

"No!" Gitana exclaimed, extending her arm as if to ward

him off and glancing at the open door. She lowered her voice and went on rapidly. "Not now, *por favor*. Later, after we have eaten, I will pay you a visit."

Fargo went to grab her, then hesitated. Perhaps she had a point. It wouldn't do to have her father blunder upon them while they were glued to one another; the poor man's heart might give out right then and there. "All right," he growled reluctantly, "but I'm holding you to your word."

She grinned and gazed at the bulge in his buckskins. The tip of her tongue jutted from between her red lips. "This is one promise I will be glad to keep." She winked and dashed from the room, trailing laughter in her wake.

Feeling hungry in more ways than one, Fargo prowled the room and opened the two doors that led off from it. One connected to another bedroom, the other led into a room containing a washbowl and tub. He returned to his room, intending to go out and inquire about the availability of hot water, but drew up short in surprise at finding a young Mexican woman standing just inside the doorway.

The moment she laid eyes on him she curtsied and smiled sheepishly. Clothed in a white blouse and a full black skirt, she had her black hair tied at the back with a red ribbon.

"Who are you?" Fargo demanded.

"Pardon me, *senor*. I am Dolorita, the maid. I speak fair English. Senorita Otero told me to see to your needs."

"Oh." Fargo pointed at the bathroom. "Any chance of getting some hot water for a bath?"

"*Si, senor,*" Dolorita replied eagerly. "Hot water. *Pronto*, yes?" She spun on her slender heels and hastened off to fulfill his request.

Fargo strolled to a window and stared down at the stable. He saw Reyes Feliz talking with three *vaqueros*, one of whom wore a white sombrero. The trio appeared angry. Feliz was gesturing forcefully as if stressing a point. After watching them for a minute, he stretched, went to the bed, and sat down.

Tomorrow he would commence his campaign against the Apaches. The first order of business was to track them to their lair. Once he located their village, he could plot a strategy for driving them out of the valley.

He thought of the wounded warrior he'd encountered—the

33

one on the horse bearing the fine Spanish saddle—and wondered if the man had died. He regretted not having taken the horse since it undoubtedly belonged to the Oteros and they would have been grateful to get it back.

Fargo heard the patter of footsteps in the hall and a second later the maid appeared. She hesitated in the doorway as if afraid to enter until he beckoned her in. He couldn't help but notice that although Dolorita wasn't a stunning beauty like Gitana Otero, she was exceptionally attractive in her own right. "Is the water on the way?" he asked.

"*Si, senor.* In ten minutes it will be very ready." She paused. "Sorry. Was that proper English?"

"It's good enough," Fargo informed her, studying her features. Her frank gaze persuaded him that she was an honest sort who just might be a useful source of information. "How long have you been working for the Otero family?"

"Two years, *senor,*" Dolorita said, and moved toward the doorway. "I must be going."

"Hold on there, *senorita*. I'd like to talk to you about your work here."

Dolorita blinked, then vigorously shook her head. "I have other work to do. I must go." With that she whirled and raced out like a spooked doe fleeing from a ravenous mountain lion.

Now what was that all about? Fargo mused. She gave him the impression of being afraid to talk about her employers. Why? Was she under specific orders from Gitana or Celestino? He sat in a chair reflecting on the strange state of affairs until a pair of servants, neither of whom was Dolorita, brought the hot water up from the kitchen.

A pleasant, leisurely bath, the first he'd enjoyed in many a moon, relaxed him and made him feel like a new man when he ventured downstairs for supper after being summoned by a man in a black suit. The dining room was enormous, dominated by a long, polished mahogany table in the center of the room.

The only ones dining were the Oteros and himself. He sat on the father's right hand, with Gitana directly across from him, and listened to the beauty translate her father's account of how it was back in the old days when the Otero family first moved to Mexico from Spain. The talk bored him. But halfway through the delicious meal of various Mexican dishes including enchiladas, tostadas, tamales, and atole, his interest perked up.

He was about to take a sip of cinnamon-flavored hot chocolate when he felt soft pressure on his right shin and something slid up and down his leg. Looking over the rim of his cup he noticed a slight smirk creasing Gitana's lips as her toes traced a path from his knee to his ankle. He went on eating and listening while she sensuously rubbed his legs.

Fargo learned nothing new during the meal until they were eating dessert. Gitana, preoccupied with stroking him, was absently translating every remark her father made.

"I hope you can succeed where so many others have failed," she stated on her father's behalf. "The Apaches must be eliminated. After dealing with them all my life, I am eager to end this affair once and for all."

Busily chewing, it took Fargo a moment for his words to sink in. Then he glanced at Gitana. "He's dealt with them all of his life? I thought you told me the Chiricahuas showed up here about four years ago?"

Gitana gazed from her father to the Trailsman. "They did. My apologies if I failed to translate properly. What my father really said was that after living here all of his life, he's eager to have the valley be peaceful again."

Fargo resumed eating. Her explanation made sense, but the comment only added fuel to his smoldering suspicion that things weren't as they seemed. He was glad when the meal finally concluded.

Standing, Gitana spoke with her father, then grinned at Fargo. "Would you be so kind as to join me on the portico for some refreshing air?"

"Why not?"

She led the way along a corridor to a set of double doors on the west side of the house. The large porch afforded a magnificent view of the rugged mountains bordering the valley and the resplendent hues of the setting sun. Thirty yards away was the bunkhouse. In between were a few high trees.

"Did you enjoy your meal?" Gitana asked as she sank into a chair, her white dress rustling with her movements.

"Never had better," Fargo said, stepping over to lean against a column. A cool westerly breeze fanned his face and he inhaled deeply.

"I trust it hasn't made you too tired?"

Her meaning was obvious. Fargo glanced at the firebrand. "Nothing could make me *that* tired, ma'am."

"How nice."

For a while they said nothing as the sun sank from sight and the gray twilight began to give way to twinkling stars and the inkiness of nightfall. In the house, servants were busy going from room to room lighting lamps. Off in the distance a coyote howled. Close at hand an owl hooted.

Another owl answered from a tree on the left.

Fargo instantly straightened, his right hand dropping to his Colt. That last hoot hadn't emanated from the branches, where any self-respecting owl would naturally perch, but rather from behind the tree trunk. No sooner did he come to that conclusion when the night blossomed with blasting fire and slugs smacked into the column at his side.

5

Gitana heaved out of the chair, her voice raised in a strident cry: "Skye! The Apaches!"

"Stay low!" Fargo bellowed, moving toward her, drawing on the run. Another shot cracked from the tree shielding the false owl. He fired, aiming at the flash, unable to tell if he hit or missed. In four bounds he reached Gitana, who had crouched next to the chair, and snapped off two more shots.

There were shouts from the grounds and within the *hacienda*. Servants emerged, their *patron* with them and armed with a rifle. From the bunkhouse spilled *vaqueros*, revolvers at the ready, who moved toward the great house.

Fargo stood in front of Gitana, protecting her with his own body, and scanned the yard. There had been at least two assassins out there but now he saw no sign of anyone other than the onrushing *vaqueros*, some of whom were carrying lanterns. He let himself relax a bit and lowered the Colt.

Celestino Otero came directly to his daughter and embraced her. She related the details of the attack.

Reyes Feliz was one of the first *vaqueros* on the scene. He glowered at the Trailsman and went over to the Oteros, listening intently to Gitana's recital. When she finished, he issued instructions to the waiting *vaqueros* who promptly fanned out to search the grounds.

"Those savages will stop at nothing," Gitana spat, looking at Fargo. "Now we can't even sit outside in the cool of the evening."

Twirling the .44 into its holster, Fargo tried to keep the anger out of his tone as he said, "It's a mite peculiar that they were using guns. The Apaches you tangled with today weren't using firearms."

"They have stolen a few from the *vaqueros* they've killed,"

37

Gitana disclosed. "Fortunately, they are pathetic shots."

Fargo had never heard tell of an Apache being a pathetic marksman. Indians relied on their hunting skills to stay alive. Whether using bows or guns, all warriors invariably became competent enough to hit any target nine times out of ten.

"My father apologizes for not having posted guards," Gitana translated. "He wants you to know there will be a dozen men around the house all night long."

"I'll sleep a heap better."

Celestino ushered them into the sitting room. Through his daughter he offered his guest a drink.

"No thanks," Fargo declined. If someone was out to kill him, he wanted a clear head at all times. Guards or no guards, he wasn't taking any chances. "In fact," he went on, "it's been a long day and I'm tuckered out. I think I'll turn in."

"So early?" Gitana asked in surprise.

"I want to start at the crack of dawn tomorrow," Fargo told her. "I'm planning to go up into the mountains to find the Apache village." He nodded at her father and departed, taking the stairs three at a stride. As he neared his door, which was slightly ajar, he saw a shadow flit across the narrow opening. Wrapping his fingers around the butt of his Colt, he crept to the door, then shoved it open with the toe of his left boot.

Standing on the far side next to a dresser near the window, lighting the second of two lamps that illuminated the bedroom, was the maid. Dolorita whirled, her hand covering her mouth. Then she recognized him and sighed in relief. "*Senor*, you scare me, yes? After all that shooting . . ." she said, and shuddered.

Entering, Fargo crossed his arms and regarded her severely. "I never expected to see you in here again after the way you acted earlier."

She bowed her head. "I am most sorry, *senor*."

"Can we talk now? I'd still like to know a few things."

"No," Dolorita said and made for the doorway.

Fargo grabbed her arm as he went past and held fast. She turned fearful eyes on him and tugged to get free.

"Please, *senor*."

"I just want you to know I'm your friend," Fargo assured her, careful not to squeeze too hard. "You can trust me."

"I trust no one," Dolorita declared, glancing at the hallway.

Frowning, the big man released her and watched her dash from the chamber. Why was she so afraid to talk to him? What did she know? He resolved to try to get the information out of her later. For now, he felt truly fatigued. Closing the door, he removed his hat and buckskin shirt and placed both on top of the dresser. The .44 went under the large, fluffy pillow on which he would sleep. Should anyone decide to pay him an unwanted visit in the middle of the night, they'd be in for a nasty shock.

He sat on the edge of the bed and pulled the Arkansas toothpick from his right boot. The finely crafted knife, with its long and sharply tapering blade, had gotten him out of many a scrape. He slipped the dagger under the other pillow where it would be handy in an emergency. Then he reclined on his back, placing his right hand under the first pillow and nestling his hand around the Colt.

Since, like Dolorita, he couldn't trust anyone, he elected to leave both lamps burning. The light might discourage anyone tempted to try to sneak into his room. He pondered the many events of the hectic day, striving to make sense of the contradictions. His eyelids closed, and before he knew it sleep claimed him.

A lifetime of living on the raw edge of the frontier had endowed the Trailsman with the uncanny instincts of a wary mountain lion, and so it was that at the very moment the soft rustle of a garment reached his ears he came instantly awake. He lay still, pretending to be asleep, and cracked his eyes for a peek.

Just coming through the doorway connecting his bedroom to the next was Gitana Otero, her full figure clad in a sheer white nightgown that clung suggestively to her body. She closed the door behind her and glanced in annoyance at both lamps. Gazing at him, she broke into a grin and tiptoed over to the bed.

Fargo continued to feign sleep, amused at her antics. She slid into the bed and crawled ever so slowly up to his side. Lying on her right side, she stared at his groin and hungrily licked her lips. It took all of his self-control to stop himself from bursting into laughter.

Gitana leaned over and lightly pecked him on the cheek. She gently nibbled lower, letting her tongue touch the soft flesh of his neck. Grinning impishly, she placed her left hand on his chest and let her hand roam at will.

Feeling his manhood surge to attention, Fargo watched her hand slide down to the top of his pants. Her warm breath on his face as her fingers eased under his buckskins aroused him intensely. He waited until her probing fingers found what they were after and heard her intake of breath when she grasped him.

"Like what you've found?" Fargo asked, opening his eyes.

She swallowed and nodded, tracing a finger along the length of his shaft. Suddenly she blinked and looked at his face. "You bastard. You've been awake this whole time."

"And enjoying every second," Fargo said, smirking. He took her into his arms and planted a lingering kiss on her pliant lips. Their bodies melded together and she let go of his organ to run her hands all over him.

Fargo cupped her left breast, eliciting a moan of stark passion that welled up from deep in her throat. He switched to the other swelling mound and squeezed. She strained against him, the heat of her body enough to scorch her garment.

He broke the kiss to reach down and pull the nightgown up above her breasts. Her taut nipples jiggled inches from his lips, a temptation too sweet to resist. His mouth closed on first one, then the other, his tongue swirling each tip while she cooed and squirmed.

"Oh, Skye," Gitana said huskily, her eyes partially closed. She twined her fingers into his hair and mashed his greedy mouth against her breasts.

Fargo traced his tongue along her ribs, from one side to the other, until he came to her navel. The musky scent rising from between her legs tingled in his nostrils and he moved lower.

"Oh, yes. Oh, yes," Gitana panted. She parted her legs to grant him access to her nether parts and arched her spine when his mouth found her steaming tunnel. "Ahhhh. So good. Keep going. Don't stop."

Her legs quivered uncontrollably while her buttocks bounced with every lick. Her incredibly smooth thighs closed on either side of his head, enveloping him in their warmth.

"Magnifico!" Gitana said. She seized him by the hair and jerked his head up. "Please! I want you inside me. I'm burning up."

The big man hastily stripped off his pants and moccasins, knelt between her legs, and slowly eased into her. Her slick cavity seemed to close around his shaft, accommodating him in a silken sheath, and suddenly she went crazy, her hips bucking like a wild mare as she whined and reached for him. He pressed his chest to her mounds and glued his lips to hers.

His powerful legs and stomach muscles drove him in and out, in and out, arousing her to a fever pitch. She mewed and heaved to match his strokes, sweat making both of them slick, their bellies slapping together rhythmically. On and on they went. Finally, unable to hold back any longer, he spurted violently into her and felt her shudder convulsively in response.

"Ooooooh. Oh, God!" she exclaimed.

They coasted to an eventual stop with Fargo resting on her chest. Both of them inhaled deeply, satiated by their mutual release. He kissed her again and eased onto his side.

"You made me want to scream," Gitana said dreamily, snuggling into his shoulder.

"Why didn't you?" Fargo responded in jest.

"And have my poor *padre* hear?" Gitana expelled an unladylike snort. "Such a shock might kill him."

They lay quietly, savoring the moment, until Gitana turned her face up to his.

"Oh. By the way. Our men found no trace of the Apaches who shot at us."

"I'm not surprised."

"They searched the entire grounds and every building but the savages had vanished like ghosts in the night. You know how Apaches are. They leave no tracks and can melt into the ground."

"You've been listening to too many wild tales," Fargo said. "Everyone leaves tracks, even Apaches. They don't leave many, but a good tracker can follow their sign."

"They say you are the best."

"Who says?"

"Some of our men. Even here in this remote valley we have

41

heard of the Trailsman," Gitana said, studying his face. "That *is* what they call you?"

"Some do," Fargo admitted. He didn't bother to mention that the handle could be a mixed blessing. The mere mention of the name sometimes served to intimidate hardcases who might otherwise be inclined to give him trouble. Then, too, there were those yacks who wanted to make a big name for themselves and felt the best way to do so was to gun down someone with a widespread reputation—someone like the Trailsman.

"If anyone can end our Apache problem, it's you," Gitana predicted confidently. "Just remember, Skye. The savages aren't to be trusted. Shoot them on sight or you'll live to regret it."

"I know how to take care of myself," he said testily.

"You certainly do," Gitana agreed, grinning from ear to ear. She kissed his neck and ran her fingers over his chest. "I only regret our foreman did not hire you sooner."

"Which reminds me. Who do I talk to about the gold I've been promised? The deal calls for a gold coin a day until the job is done."

"I know all about the price of your services. I was the one who suggested such an amount to my father before Rojos even left for Tucson. We had tried everything else. We offered currency, horses, even a few choice parcels of land to men with the courage to take the fight to the Apaches. There were none. Using gold coins was our last resort."

Fargo saw an opening and took advantage of it. Keeping his voice calm, he innocently asked, "And what about Feliz? Don't tell me he came cheap."

The firebrand seemed to stiffen. "Nothing escapes your notice, does it? No, Reyes did not come cheaply. Rojos found him in Sante Fe six months ago and made him a lucrative offer. Believe me, Reyes has proven himself worth every *centavo*," Gitana said. "Unfortunately, he's no tracker. His skill lies elsewhere."

"In killing," Fargo said flatly.

"Why do you resent him so? If not for Reyes, the rest of the *vaqueros* might have left months ago. He gives them hope and fills them with confidence. He's kept them working for us."

The remark made Fargo wonder. Were the *vaqueros* staying because Feliz inspired them or because they were afraid his deadly skill with a *pistola* might be turned on them should they try to abandon the Oteros?

Gitana sat up abruptly and pulled her nightgown down. "As much as I would like to spend the night with you, I must be going. If I should miss seeing you in the morning, please know my thoughts will be with you." She climbed off the bed and smiled at him. "I gave instructions to have your pinto saddled and waiting out front at first light. I also ordered the cook to get some *tasajo*—jerked beef—ready for you."

"Thanks."

"It's the least I can do. You're risking your life to save our ranch. I want to do everything I can to show my appreciation."

Fargo's eyes roved over her voluptuous figure. "I'd say you're doing a first-rate job."

6

The sun was just peeking above the eastern horizon when the Trailsman swung into the saddle and rode from the *hacienda*. Already many of the field hands and *vaqueros* were up and around. He spotted Reyes Feliz near the bunkhouse, watching him leave. Beside the *pistolero* were the three men Feliz had been talking to so earnestly the day before. All four glared at him openly.

Fargo stuck to the road that bisected the vast estate from east to west. He glanced back repeatedly to see if anyone would be foolhardy enough to shadow him, but no one appeared other than a few hands about to begin a hard day's labor tilling the crops. He adjusted the Sharps' holster so the stock was within easy reach and surveyed the terrain ahead.

Beyond the fields and the cattlerange loomed an arm of the Santa Maria chain, an isolated mountain range completely untouched by the westward creep of white civilization and the cultivated hands of Spaniards and Mexicans alike. If the Apaches had a village near the valley, Fargo reasoned, it would be located in those mountains.

To the south lay land that had once been regularly patrolled by Mexican *federales,* and even though Mexico no longer possessed the region, the Chiricahuas had a long memory and wouldn't take the risk of establishing a village there. To the north was a region frequently visited by mountain men and prospectors. Again, the Chiricahuas would avoid it like the plague. And although the land to the east between the valley and Santa Fe was sparsely inhabited, the territory was criss-crossed regularly by cavalry patrols and others.

No, Fargo mused, the village had to be to the west, possibly the northwest. He knew how the Apache mind worked, knew they often acted contrary to what they believed their enemies would expect. And he recollected that yesterday the warriors had ridden off to the southeast after the battle at the pass. If his hunch was right, then the Chiricahuas had deliberately gone in the opposite direction of their village in case the *vaqueros* had followed.

The sun warmed him as he rode. He enjoyed the mild breeze on his face and the rolling motion of the stallion. In due course he left the last of the cattle behind. An hour elapsed. Then two. It wasn't until the sun hung at the midday position that he reached the base of the foothills rising toward the stark peaks a bit farther west.

The road ended. He angled to the northwest, scanning the ground in all directions. To his surprise, he found a number of tracks made by shod horses, evidently from the *hacienda*. Most were old sign, a week or better, but he found a trail made by four mounts that had traveled to the northwest and returned approximately two days ago.

The discovery aroused his curiosity. He followed the trail even higher. The quartet had traversed the foothills and skirted a forested tract at the base of the mountain. Their tracks went along the rim of a gorge, then cut northward.

Fargo abruptly reined up and climbed down. Dropping to his left knee, his keen lake-blue eyes examined the ground intently. There could be no mistake. Imprinted in the soil, as clear as the nose on his face, were the tracks of three Indian horses. As incredible as it seemed, the three Indians had met the four riders from the *hacienda* at that very spot. Then the quartet had headed for the valley and the trio of Chiricahuas had retraced their steps to the north.

What did it all mean? Perplexed, Fargo mounted and stayed with the trail made by the Apaches. In half a mile the tracks changed direction, going westward. All around him were twisting spires of rock and monoliths carved from solid stone. The ground itself was almost too hard to record prints and he had to slow down in order not to miss any critical sign.

Soon he came to a small spring at the base of low cliff and stopped. He let the Ovaro drink and removed the packet of jerked beef from his saddle bag. As he ate he mulled the implications of his discovery. He'd been led to believe the

Apaches killed the *vaqueros* and others on sight. Why, then, had some sort of parley been arranged?

A strident screech sounded overhead as a large hawk soared by on the air currents.

Fargo stretched, took a bite of jerky, and froze when the stallion suddenly pricked its ears and stared at a jumble of boulders off to the right, its nostrils flaring. He'd learned to rely on the Ovaro's instincts, and he did so now by dropping the jerky and springing into the saddle. With a snap of the reins he wheeled the big horse and rode to the west, making for the shelter of a rearing spire, his head twisted to observe the rocks.

Venting fierce whoops, two mounted Apaches burst from the boulders and galloped in pursuit. Both carried bows, arrows already nocked to their strings.

Whipping the reins, Fargo brought the pinto to its top speed. He felt confident he could easily outrun the warriors and would rather do so than use a gun since any gunshots would carry for a considerable distance and might alert other Chiricahuas in the vicinity. But a moment later he had no choice.

From around the spire appeared a third Apache, this one carrying a war club. He voiced a war whoop and bore down on the Trailsman, the club upraised.

Fargo's right hand swept the .44 up and out. He squeezed off a shot when only fifteen feet separated them, and the impact flung the warrior over the back of his horse to crash onto the earth. Hunching over the saddle, Fargo kept going.

An arrow streaked out of the blue, narrowly missing his left shoulder.

No one knew better than Fargo how adept Indians were with bows. No matter the tribe, most warriors learned to shoot accurately at an early age. Some, such as the Sioux and the Comanches, taught their boys to shoot from horseback when the youngsters were a mere six or seven. And while a bow might lack the range of a Sharps or a Hawken, in the hands of a skilled archer an arrow could be fired accurately up to one hundred yards. Not only that, but some warriors could unleash six or seven shafts in the span of a minute.

His spine tingling, expecting to receive a barbed point in the back at any second, Fargo slanted toward a narrow gap between two immense boulders. Another arrow zipped past on the right.

He looked back and saw the two warriors unleash shafts simultaneously. Glinting in the sunlight, the spinning harbingers of death arced dead on target.

He tracked their flight and waited until the very last instant before angling slightly to the right. Both arrows cleaved the space the stallion had just vacated and thudded into the soil. Correcting his course, he made a beeline to the gap and clattered through it twenty yards ahead of the Apaches.

Fargo brought the pinto around and leveled the Colt. The first Indian to come through never knew what hit him; a hole blossomed in his forehead and he fell sideways. The second man, alerted, was trying to swing to the off side of his mount when the .44 blasted and lead ripped through his throat. Spraying crimson, the Apache tumbled.

He watched the second warrior convulse violently before dying, then reloaded the Colt and turned to the northwest. If luck was with him, their village was far enough away that the shots hadn't been heard. If not, he'd be up to his neck in bloodthirsty devils in no time.

Unfortunately, he'd now lost the sign he'd been following, which meant he must locate the village another way. Repeatedly glancing along his backtrail, he pressed on for almost an hour before bringing the Ovaro to a halt on a rise that commanded a panoramic view of the surrounding countryside.

To the west and south were steep mountains, to the north a vast plateau connected to the rise by a narrow strip of land, an earthen bridge sharply eroded on both sides. Acting on his previous hunch, he rode to the bridge, a span no more than six feet wide, and gingerly moved the stallion out onto it. The big horse behaved skittishly until he bent down, patted its neck, and spoke softly into its ear.

Reassured, the stallion walked forward without a qualm. The wind picked up, whipping the pinto's mane and threatening to tear Fargo's hat from his head. He pulled it down tighter and squared his broad shoulders. The span narrowed to only four feet in width near the center and the Ovaro slowed but kept going.

Fargo could see boulders far below on both sides. He licked his dry lips and let the stallion take its own sweet time. A misstep now would plunge both of them to certain death. Not until they were close to the plateau did he feel the tension drain from his body.

He picked up the pace, encouraged by what he saw. The top of the plateau was heavily forested, with ponderosa pine, blue spruce, and Douglas fir growing in profusion. There was also ample grass. The vegetation indicated there must be a constant water source, and both combined meant there must be plenty of game about. He nodded in satisfaction. If the Apaches knew about this plateau—and the odds were they did—then this was where they would establish their village.

The Trailsman rode into the trees to minimize the risk of being spotted from afar and cautiously headed northward. The woods were alive with the chirping of various birds and the chattering of squirrels. Once he glimpsed a deer fleeing into the undergrowth.

He'd gone barely half a mile when his nostrils detected the faint aroma of smoke. Stopping, he sniffed the air, marking the direction of the breeze which was blowing from the northwest to the southeast. Swinging northwest, he went slowly toward the source of the smoke. Before long he heard the sound of voices and the laughter of children at play.

Fargo halted beside a log and swung down. After securing the reins to a tree limb, he took the Sharps and advanced on foot. Staying low, using every available cover, he covered another hundred yards, then heard a loud laugh near at hand and crouched behind a Douglas fir to survey the countryside ahead.

Another ten yards of forest remained. Beyond the trees lay a meadow. At its center was a small, placid lake, and on the western shore were the lodges of the Chiricahua Apaches. Constructed by first erecting a conical framework of slender poles, then covering the frame with interwoven brush and grass, such dwellings were admirably weather resistant, well ventilated in hot weather, and easy to repair.

Fargo counted twenty-one wickiups, as some whites called them. A number of campfires were blazing as women busied themselves at preparing food. Happy children were scattered about the village, playing heartily. Horses were tethered at various points. There were also a few dogs in evidence.

The latter bothered Fargo. Their keen sense of smell and sharp hearing made them perfect guards, and he had to be diligent to avoid giving his presence away. As his eyes roved over the village he realized very few warriors were there, possibly because the rest had ridden off to investigate the faint shots undoubtedly heard when he fought those three men near the spring.

He flattened, held his elbows bent with the Sharps clenched firmly in both hands, and crawled forward. He wanted to spy on the village for a spell, learn everything he could about the tribe. A patch of waist-high weeds bordering the forest provided the ideal place to hide and observe. Placing the rifle at his side, he carefully parted the grass until he could see clearly and settled down to spend hours there, if necessary.

A strange fact struck him. Nearly all of the women he saw were elderly, in their fifties or better. And of the few warriors in the village, all of them except two were also advanced in years, many with white hair. He could account for the absence of the young men because most were probably out hunting for whoever had killed their fellows—for him. But where were the majority of young women?

Mystified, Fargo saw a notable exception: a lovely woman in her twenties emerged from a lodge and walked toward the lake, a large clay jug in her arms. She wore a beaded buckskin dress that swayed with every step she took. Her luxurious black hair fell to the small of her back. Without a doubt she qualified as the prettiest woman in the entire village.

Engrossed in admiring her, Fargo had no idea he was in any immediate danger until he heard a low yip and glanced to his left to discover a pair of camp dogs were heading in his direction. He stayed as still as a rock, hoping they wouldn't notice him.

The dogs, both big mongrels, were sniffing the ground and walking side-by-side. They drew up well shy of the grass and one began moving in a circle.

Fargo guessed they were on the scent of a rabbit or some such critter that had ventured near the village. Whatever the case might be, in another fifteen feet they would surely spot him and bark furiously to alert their masters. His best bet would be to sneak into the trees and get away before anyone came to investigate. If the dogs pursued him, his throwing knife would come in real handy.

The dog moving in the circle started swinging ever wider and came nearer, its nose just above the ground, oblivious to everything but the matter at hand.

Tensing, Fargo saw the animal pause and glance up. It stared directly at him and he felt certain the dog saw him. Oddly, the mongrel gazed past him, wagged its tail a few times, then abruptly wheeled and ran back into the village with its companion in tow.

Thank goodness dogs were unpredictable, Fargo reflected, relieved at his narrow escape. He gazed at the attractive woman again, observing her fill the jug, when suddenly something dawned on him.

Dogs seldom wagged their tails for the hell of it. Tail wagging was a gesture of devotion or friendship, usually done when the animal in question saw someone it was fond of or at least knew. And that dog had been looking at something—or someone— behind him.

A dreadful premonition gripped him and he twisted to glance over his right shoulder. His blood ran cold at the sight of four hardy Apaches creeping up on him, each carrying a war club. Even as he laid eyes on them, they charged.

7

Trying to employ the Colt would be foolhardy; the warriors were too close. Fargo had no recourse but to surge erect and swing the Sharps around. The blast would arouse the Indians in the village, but it couldn't be helped. His thumb, though, was just pulling the hammer back when the foremost Apache swung his club and battered the barrel aside.

Before Fargo could compensate, the warrior was on him, raising the club for another strike. He pivoted and slammed the Sharps' stock into the man's face, staggering him, then whipped the heavy barrel across the Chiricahua's brow. The Indian dropped.

In a flash the remaining three converged on him, and it was all Fargo could do to stay alive. He countered a fierce swing with the rifle barrel, blocking the descending club, and shifted to face another attacker. In so doing he exposed his left side to the third warrior who promptly slammed his stone-headed war club into Fargo's arm above the elbow.

He frantically back-pedaled to give himself room to maneuver, his left arm going completely numb and useless. Letting go of the Sharps, he swooped his right hand to the .44 and began to clear leather.

One of the Apaches, the tallest and most muscular of the lot, suddenly snapped his right arm back, then forward, throwing his club at the Trailsman's head.

Fargo ducked to the left but was struck a glancing blow on the right temple. Dazed, he nonetheless managed to clear leather and leveled the Colt to fire.

Pouncing like cougars, the three warriors were on him before he could shoot. One looped his arms around Fargo's chest, another grabbed his legs. The third seized his gun arm and held fast.

Fargo buckled under their combined weight, going to his

knees. With his left arm out of commission and his right in the grip of an enemy, all he could do was drive his forehead into the upturned face of the Apache clinging to his chest. He felt the man's nose give way and heard a crunch. Then they bore him to the ground.

Fargo struggled as best he could, to no avail. They were intent on holding him there and made no attempt to employ their war clubs again. With a start he realized they were trying to take him alive. The thought made his blood race. He forced his left arm to move, driving his fist into the abdomen of the man on his chest. The warrior's grip slackened. A second punch caused the Apache to slip off, clutching his stomach.

It was now or never. Fargo kicked and bucked while struggling to his knee. He dislodged the Chiricahua holding his legs and turned to pummel the warrior still clinging to his gun arm. At that moment something smashed into the back of his head. Bright pinpoints of light exploded before his eyes and dizziness assailed him. He reeled, reached out for support that wasn't there, and barely felt the second blow that sent his consciousness swirling into a bottomless black void.

Fargo became aware of pain, excruciating pain that made his head throb terribly. In a rush, memories of the fight reminded him of the reason for his agony. He kept his eyes closed, taking stock. Both his wrists and ankles were tightly bound and he was lying on his right side. But where?

Suddenly there was a commotion and the sound of voices, a man and a woman speaking in the Chiricahua tongue.

He listened, unable to understand a word they said other than their term for "white man," and heard them come closer until they were standing right beside him. The warriors must have carted him into the village. Since he felt no breeze but could hear the muted barking of a dog, he deduced they had placed him in a lodge.

The conversation ended and soft footfalls moved away. Fargo heard rustling, then a cool hand touched his cheek. Probing fingers examined the back of his head. He detected a pleasant scent that reminded him of fresh flowers and cracked his eyelids.

Kneeling in front of him, her brow knit as she ran her fingers through his hair, was the attractive Indian woman who had filled the jug at the lake. Her lips were just above his face, the full contours of her chest only an inch away. She straightened, her penetrating dark eyes regarding him intently. Then she addressed him in her own language.

Fargo couldn't understand why she would speak to someone she believed to be unconscious. She reached out, tapped him on the tip of the nose, and spoke coldly. It dawned on him that she knew he was awake. How? Had the rhythm of his breathing changed drastically? Realizing that playing possum would accomplish nothing, he opened his eyes.

The woman simply stared for a minute, unflinchingly meeting his gaze. Her mouth curled contemptuously and she snapped what sounded like a question.

"I don't understand," Fargo said. "Do you speak English?"

Apparently puzzled, the woman responded in Chiricahua. She gestured at the lodge entrance for emphasis.

Fargo shook his head. He tried Sioux, then used a little Spanish. The former elicited no reaction whatsoever, but she reacted to the latter by angrily raising her right hand in front of her right shoulder, her hand nearly closed, and then sweeping the hand down and to the left, stopping suddenly with a jerking motion. He understood perfectly. She'd just used Indian sign language for the word "kill." But what did she mean? Did she want to kill all Spanish-speaking people? He nodded at her hand and said, "Sign. Yes. *Si. Si.*"

Her forehead creased and she looked at her hand in confusion. Suddenly comprehension lit her face and she moved both arms swiftly, her fingers flying, asking a question. "Can you talk in sign language, white man?"

Since his own arms were bound, the best Fargo could do was nod vigorously and grin like an idiot. "Yes, I speak sign," he assured her.

She appeared to grasp the gist of his reply and abruptly stood. Spinning on her heel, her long hair flying, she hastened from the lodge.

Fargo had an opportunity to take stock. There were several blankets and robes piled in one corner. On another side were bowls and baskets. But there were no weapons of any sort. The

Apaches must have removed anything and everything that he could use to free himself or against them prior to dumping him inside.

He didn't have long to wait before the maiden returned, and she didn't come alone. The same tall, muscular warrior he'd fought at the edge of the forest came with her, as did two other men he hadn't seen before. They entered and paused, the men giving him spiteful looks, until the tall one barked directions. The other two stepped forward. Each grabbed one of Fargo's arms, and the next moment he was rudely wrenched to his feet.

The tall warrior's hands moved. "My sister tells me you speak sign language?"

"Yes," Fargo answered, nodding his head and hoping the Chiricahua would perceive his meaning.

Striding nearer, the tall man issued more commands. His two companions promptly produced long knives. In short, precise strokes they slashed the rope binding the Trailsman's wrists and ankles, then stood back with their blades held at the ready. At the slightest hostile move, they would strike.

Fargo rubbed his wrists and slowly lifted his legs to restore the circulation. Now that he was upright he could feel the Arkansas toothpick snug in his right boot. The Apaches hadn't noticed it when binding him; evidently they hadn't bothered to lift his pant leg. He smiled at the woman to show his appreciation for her insight in getting the warriors, but her features might as well have been chiseled from stone for all the reaction she displayed.

The tall Chiricahua grunted and posed a demand. "Prove that you speak sign."

"What would you have me say?" Fargo signed back, his arms a bit sluggish. He must have been out for quite some time.

All four Apaches exchanged glances.

"How are you called, white man?" asked the tall one.

Fargo didn't bother to try and present his given name in sign. While there was a sign gesture for the word "sky," there was none for Fargo. Instead, he used a combination of signs to tell them, "I am known as the Trailsman."

"Nana," the tall Chiricahua said, tapping his chest. He studied Fargo intently, then used sign. "You have the look about

54

you of one who has lived much as we do. Are you one of those whites who has lived among one of the tribes?"

"Yes," Fargo admitted, admiring the man's insight. "I have spent time with several."

"This is good," Nana signed. "Then you will better understand our ways. We have much to talk over. But first I want you to promise that you will not try to escape if I leave you untied."

Fargo was surprised but didn't let it show. Only a man of honor, white or otherwise, would make such an offer. If he gave his word, he would be obligated to stick by it. "I will not try to escape until we have finished our talk," he replied.

Nana grinned, then nodded at his sister. "Nalin," he introduced her. His hands moved. "She tells me your head must be hurting very badly. After she has brought herbs for the pain, we will talk more." So saying, he wheeled and departed with the two other warriors in tow.

Nalin smiled sheepishly. "I will return soon," she signed, and ran out.

Fargo stepped to the entrance, trying to make sense of it all. He saw the sun suspended above the western horizon. Darkness would soon descend. He also saw many more men in the village now, most of them on the elderly side. Off to his right, near another wickiup, stood the very stallion he'd seen near the pass, the one bearing the fine Spanish saddle. Apparently the wounded warrior had returned safely.

He reached in back of his head and gingerly probed with his fingers, discovering a nasty gash several inches long. No wonder he hurt like the dickens. A bit deeper and he might never have revived.

In less than two minutes Nalin came back carrying a bowl containing herbs, a jug of water, and a cloth. She motioned for him to sit, then moved behind him.

Fargo admitted her delicacy as she worked. Never once did she intentionally cause additional pain. Whatever she used stung terribly but he stoically bore up. When she was done, she came around in front of him, her hands empty.

"You must be careful not to get dirt on your head. Wash your wound in the lake tomorrow and every day after that. In one moon you will be healed completely."

"Thank you. How can I repay your kindness?" Fargo asked.

"You already have," she answered.

"How is that possible?"

"You will know shortly."

The big man stood and reclaimed his hat. He eased it onto his head, the band slightly increasing the pressure on his wound but not to the point where he couldn't tolerate the discomfort. Amazement registered on Nalin's face and she made a clucking sound with her tongue.

"I will never understand why white men wear such ridiculous things on their heads," she remarked. "And now even some of our people have taken to doing it."

"White women wear hats also," Fargo informed her. "Their hats are even more ridiculous."

Nalin giggled. She smoothed her dress with her palms and glanced at the doorway, seeming nervous about being alone with him, then used sign. "My brother will return soon." She paused. "He told me you fought bravely today. He said you have the strength of three men."

"Why did your brother take me alive?" Fargo queried. "He could easily have killed me."

"He will explain everything," she assured him.

At that moment her brother's powerful frame filled the entrance. He smiled at her and came over to the Trailsman. "You should know that your horse is being well taken care of. Your rifle and pistol are both in my lodge and may be given back to you depending on our chief's decision."

"Who is your chief?"

"Chihuahua," Nana stated, and led the way outside.

Fargo dutifully followed. Many members of the tribe had gathered near the lodge. Whispered conversations erupted among them as he appeared. Some cast hateful gazes in his direction, others were merely curious. He discovered Nana was heading straight for the lodge where the Spanish mount stood tethered.

Suddenly three warriors broke away from the crowd and moved to intercept Nana. They halted and the foremost Apache, a stocky man whose face was contorted in a perpetual scowl, growled out a series of harsh sentences.

Nana listened impatiently. He responded firmly and went to move past the trio but the stocky warrior blocked his path.

Other warriors converged, some standing beside Nana, most behind the belligerent Chiricahua. An argument ensued, with the stocky man pointing repeatedly at Fargo.

The Trailsman didn't like being hemmed in by so many warriors, the majority openly hostile. He wished he knew their language. Shoving broke out. The stocky Apache gave Nana a push, then was dumped on his backside when the tall Chiricahua gave him a dose of his own medicine. Drawing a knife, the stocky one jumped up and tried to gut Nana, who nimbly sidestepped and drew his own blade. Immediately the rest of the warriors moved away to give the combatants room for their struggle.

Fargo did the same, stepping back several yards. Since Nana was the only man in the village who definitely wanted to keep his hide in one piece, he had a vested interest in the outcome of the dispute. So he was more than alarmed when he saw an Apache on the sidelines heft a tomahawk and make as if to throw it at Nana's back.

8

In all the excitement, with all eyes focused on the two warriors warily circling one another, none of the Chiricahuas noticed Fargo lean down and slip his right hand into his boot. His fingers closed on the knife hilt at the very moment that the Apache with the tomahawk drew the weapon back in preparation for tossing it. Fargo uncoiled, whipping the Arkansas toothpick from concealment and flipping the knife in a underhand throw he had practiced countless times before.

The razor-edged blade flew on target, sinking into the base of the warrior's throat up to the hilt. Shocked, the Apache staggered forward, blood spraying from his ruptured jugular and spurting from the corners of his mouth. He gasped, then screeched at the top of his lungs.

All interest in the brewing fight ended. Everyone swung toward the stricken man. Even Nana and the stocky warrior paused and glanced in the direction of the sound.

Tottering to his knees, the tomahawk wielder finally let go of the weapon and feebly clutched at the knife in his neck. He tensed, then yanked the blade out. In the process, he transformed his throat into a crimson fountain.

Suddenly the stocky Apache looked at the Trailsman, shouted a sentence, and sprang to the attack. But he only took two strides when Nana's foot flicked out, tripping him, spilling him onto his face. The stocky warrior pushed upright, livid. By then Nana had moved over to stand in front of his quarry.

Other Indians came to the stocky man's aid, most with drawn knives, clubs, or tomahawks.

A few sided with Nana.

Fargo was certain bloodshed would erupt. He saw the critically wounded man pitch onto his face. Those backing the stocky warrior became strident and argumentative. They advanced arrogantly toward Nana and company.

Just then, cleaving the air like a lance, came a firm, commanding voice that stopped the stocky warrior in his tracks. Every Indian turned toward the lodge where the Spanish horse stood, and there, framed in the doorway, was the man Fargo had encountered on the way to the pass. Only now the warrior had a strip of blanket wrapped around his chest, covering the hole on his left side. He addressed his fellow Apaches sternly, then pointed at the Trailsman.

Several warriors moved to help the man struck in the neck. The stocky Chiricahua scowled at one and all, then sheathed his knife, turned, and made for another lodge.

Nana walked over to the man on the ground. He picked up Fargo's knife, wiped the blade clean on the grass, and headed for the newcomer while motioning for the prisoner to accompany him.

Fargo didn't need any prodding. Many of the Apaches were shooting arrows at him with their eyes, leaving little doubt that if they could get their hands on real bows he'd be turned into a pincushion. He trailed Nana to the hut where the warrior with the weathered features awaited them.

Nana pointed at him. "Chihuahua," he said simply.

The chief of the tribe. Fargo realized that fate had worked in his favor. "I remember you from the battle at the eastern pass," he signed, hoping to remind the chief of the fact he hadn't shot the warrior when he could easily have done so.

Chihuahua nodded and said in strongly accented English, "I remember you, white man. You are welcome in my lodge. Enter." He moved inside to the middle of the floor and sat down with a grimace.

A woman stepped from the southeast corner and knelt beside the chief. She examined the hole under the blanket, frowned, and insisted that he lie back on a blanket she provided. Chihuahua complied, reclining on his back, his shoulders propped up on a heavy robe that had been folded into a compact bundle.

Fargo moved to the right as he came inside, adhering to typical lodge etiquette for visitors. He stood beside Nana and waited for the chief to signify they could sit. As he knelt, Nana moved over to sit next to Chihuahua and the two went on at length in their own tongue.

Finally Chihuahua looked at the Trailsman. He took the Arkansas toothpick from Nana and wagged it in his hand. "You have made much trouble by using this."

"It was either that or let Nana get a tomahawk in the back," Fargo defended his action.

"So I have been told," Chihuahua said. Unexpectedly, he tossed the knife to the ground in front of the big man. "You may have need of this again."

Surprised, Fargo looked at the wounded leader. "I wish someone would explain to me just what the hell is going on."

"I will tell you all if first you will tell me some things," Chihuahua said.

"What do you want to know?"

"Why did you not kill me when you had the chance?"

"I don't make a habit out of shooting unarmed men," Fargo said. "When I saw you, you were ready to keel over at any second. I figured I'd let you die in peace."

The chief grinned. "I am sorry to disappoint you." He coughed lightly. "Tell me something else. What is your connection to the Spaniard, Otero?"

"He's hired me to work for him," Fargo said, not bothering to elaborate. He didn't believe in committing suicide.

"To kill us, you mean," Chihuahua stated harshly, and went on before the Trailsman could object. "Why else have you tracked us to our village? Why else did you sneak close to us and watch us live our lives?"

Since there was no denying the truth, Fargo kept his mouth shut. He figured if worse came to worse, if the chief decided to have him killed or Nana came to him, he could always grab the throwing knife, dash outside, and ride off on the Spanish mount before any of the Apaches could hope to stop him. He could always purchase a new Colt and Sharps.

"No matter," the chief said with a wave of his right hand. "You let me live when you could have slain me. You saved Nana. Both deeds show you to be a brave man, a man who believes in doing right. Perhaps, after I tell you our story, you will do the right thing and leave this country."

"I'm listening," Fargo said. He picked up the Arkansas toothpick and slid the knife into its sheath inside his boot.

"First, I should tell you how I know your tongue," Chihuahua said. "Many years ago, when I was young, I met a trapper who once had a cabin far north of here. I was with a war party and became separated after a raid on a Paiute village. One of the dogs hit me in the side with an arrow, and I was losing much blood. This white man, an Englishman, found me and took me to his cabin. We became friends. Once or twice a year for a dozen years I would visit him and we would teach each other our ways." He paused and frowned. "Then one day I went to his cabin and found it had been burned to the ground. The Utes had taken him."

Fargo could guess the result. During the days of the trappers and mountain men, the Utes had waged relentless war on any whites they found. "You speak our tongue well," he complimented the Apache chief.

Chihuahua gazed at the doorway. The shadows outside were lengthening as the sun set. "Enough about me. We must talk about the Spaniard, about what he has done with our people."

"I don't understand."

The chief gazed into the Trailsman's eyes for a moment. "I believe you. You don't know the truth." He shifted to make himself more comfortable. "What has the Spaniard told you about us?"

"He claims your tribe has been trying to drive him out of his valley. He says you have raided his stock, killed his hands, and attacked his house. And he's offering much money to anyone who will help him fight you."

Chihuahua took the disclosure in somber silence. "The Spaniard, as always, speaks with a forked tongue. He has lied to you, Trailsman. My people have no interest in his valley. We have been quite content in these mountains. There is plenty of water and game so our children never go hungry. And, other than the Spaniard and his men, we have no enemies."

"How long have your people lived in this region?"

"We have lost track of the years," Chihuahua said. "And until the Spaniards came, we were happy and prospered. Then the first Otero built his great house in the valley and brought in his cattle and horses and everything changed."

"In what way?"

"They started stealing our people and sending them far away where we never saw them again."

Fargo stiffened, his hands balling into fists, his memory jarred by the revelation. It was common knowledge that the early Spaniards who controlled this territory had instituted the practice of capturing Indians for use as slaves in the fields and mines of Mexico. Later, when Mexico became independent, certain wealthy Mexicans who were unwilling to give up such a cheap source of labor had continued the practice. "How long did this go on?" he inquired.

"It is still going on," Chihuahua stated.

"But that can't be," Fargo said. "This territory is now under the control of the United States."

"Tell that to Celestino Otero," the chief said bitterly. "His men still capture my people and take them south into Mexico. Already many of the young men and women have been taken. Soon they will all be gone."

Stunned, Fargo pondered the warrior's words. Now he understood the reason most of the Apaches in the village were either very young or very old. His mind balked at the notion, though. How could Otero hope to get away with such an atrocity? Then it hit him. Because the valley was situated in such a remote location and army patrols were few and far between, transporting captured Indians across the border could easily be accomplished. "I didn't know about this," he said softly.

"Now that you know, what will you do?" Chihuahua asked.

"I'm not sure," Fargo said. He pointed at the chief's chest. "How did you get that wound? What happened at the pass, anyway?"

Chihuahua's face became a mask of sorrow. "We lost good warriors that day because I was a fool." He leaned his head back and closed his eyes. "Otero sent four of his men out to find us. The one who always wears black and three others saw three of our warriors watching from a hill. The one in black used sign to get them to come closer. Then he told them that the Spaniard wanted to make peace between our peoples. Otero would show his good intentions by coming to the pass with just two men. He invited me to meet him there for a parley and to bring as many warriors as I wanted."

"What happened?" Fargo prompted when the chief stopped.

"To my shame, I went and took most of the men in our tribe. Soon a wagon came into the pass from the valley and met us

62

halfway. When I saw who was inside, I should have turned around and rode off as fast as I could. Many lives would have been saved."

Insight dawned. Fargo leaned forward and said, "It wasn't Celestino Otero."

"No. It was the daughter, and she is much worse than her father. She is like a cougar, all claws and teeth. But when she climbed from the wagon she was smiling and friendly. I thought maybe I had made a mistake," the chief said, his voice lowering to almost a whisper.

"But you hadn't?"

"No. The daughter untied a fine horse from the back of the wagon and gave it to me as a gift, to show her good will. But as soon as I climbed on the horse, her treachery was revealed. There were many of her men hidden in the rocks on the north side of the pass."

"Did they try to capture you?" Fargo asked.

"Not this time," Chihuahua said, opening his eyes and staring at the Trailsman. "They opened fire on us. I was hit and the horse ran off. Nana, my cousin, rallied our warriors and fought back. The daughter was captured as she tried to run to the men in the rocks. Two warriors were to bring her to the village, but they never showed up."

Fargo knew what had happened to them, but he wasn't telling. If Chihuahua knew how many warriors he had killed, the chief might turn against him. Besides which, he now saw the situation in the valley in a whole new light and felt guilty at having slain the Apaches without knowing the true story.

"I almost died on the way back," Chihuahua went on. "When Nana returned I told him about the strange white man who had not killed me. I described you to him." He winced and shifted again. "Earlier we heard shots and Nana took men to investigate. He found three of our warriors dead and tracked the one who had killed them. The tracks led back to our village. When he caught up to the man and saw that it was you, the one I had described, he decided to take you alive."

So now Fargo understood the reason he was still kicking. "What happens next?"

"I must hold a council. We will decide what to do with you then," the chief said. "For myself, I would let you leave without

63

harm. I owe you my life. But you killed three warriors today and there are many who would put you to death."

"Not that it's any consolation, but they were fixing to kill me."

"It doesn't matter. Mangus and others want to skin you alive and pluck out your eyes. I am not certain I can talk them into letting you live."

"Mangus is the one who argued with Nana?"

"Yes. And he hates all whites," Chihuahua said, and smiled. "He also hates all Spaniards, Mexicans, and anyone who is not Apache."

"At least he's fair about it."

"For now you will stay in the lodge Nana has given you. It belonged to one of the men you killed. Nana's sister has offered to see to your needs."

Fargo didn't much like the idea of being cooped up and at the mercy of revenge-minded Apaches who would just as soon slit his throat as spit on him. Short of trying to make a break, though, there was nothing he could do for the time being. "Any chance of getting my rifle and shooting iron back?"

The chief chuckled. "No, I am afraid not. If it is decided to let you go, all of your guns and your fine pinto will be returned to you."

"I reckon I can't ask for more," Fargo said.

Chihuahua spoke to his cousin, who stood and beckoned for the Trailsman to go with him.

Standing and striding to the entrance, Fargo paused to look back at the wounded chief. "No matter what happens next, I want to thank you now for all you've done."

"You should thank Yusn."

"Who?"

"Yusn is the Giver of Life, the one who is the source of all that is, who is above all that lives. I just try to live my life as Yusn would have me live it."

Food for thought, Fargo reflected, and nodded at the chief before stepping out into the cool evening air behind Nana. He scanned the village and spied the Ovaro tied near a lodge located twenty yards to the northeast of the one where he would bide his time until the council rendered a decision. That must be Nana's, he deduced, walking on the tall warrior's heels. When

Nana abruptly stopped a second later, he almost walked into the warrior's broad back. He looked around and instantly spotted a cause for concern.

Angrily advancing toward them was the stocky warrior named Mangus and five other Apaches.

9

"Here we go again," Fargo muttered, and stepped forward beside Nana. He wasn't going to stand idly by and twiddle his thumbs should another fight erupt.

Mangus halted a few yards off and growled a venomous string of words at Nana, who replied calmly but firmly. For a minute the argument raged. Finally, with a motion of disgust, Mangus and his companions went off toward another lodge.

Fargo continued onward when Nana did. He saw Nalin awaiting them, her anxious expression revealing her concern for her brother's safety. They talked a bit, then Nana departed.

In the Trailsman's absence Nalin had built a small fire directly under the smoke hole in the roof, then used straight tree limbs to erect a tripod that supported a deer hide cooking bag suspended over the flames. Boiling in the bag, filling the wickiup with its delicious aroma, was a bubbling stew.

Fargo leaned over the bag, sniffed loudly, and smiled at her. "I hope you will join me for the meal," he signed.

"If you want," Nalin replied, and set about arranging bowls near the fire. She glanced at him every now and then as she worked, her features inscrutable.

He took a seat and watched her, admiring her natural grace and beauty. She had a rosy glow about her typical of young Indian women. Perhaps it had something to do with living in the wild because they were always the perfect picture of health. He wondered why she had offered to cook for him and waited until she had scooped out his stew before posing the question.

Nalin paused, her cheeks flushing crimson. Then she faced him squarely, her hands and arms moving swiftly. "I do this because I love my cousin Chihuahua and he believes you are a good man." She paused and averted her gaze. "I also do this because I want to know about white men. We have heard only bad words about your kind. I would know for myself if they are true.''

"How does your husband feel about it?''

"I have no husband.''

The statement surprised Fargo. Most Indian tribes, and especially those who were noted for being warlike, such as the Apaches, suffered from a chronic shortage of men lost on raids or while hunting. To meet the constant demand for more male children, quite a few tribes indulged in letting warriors have more than one wife. Often a warrior would have three or four wives and two might be pregnant at the same time. Women were married off as soon as they came of childbearing age. For a lovely woman such as Nalin not to be married was extremely unusual.

They ate in silence. At one point Fargo heard shouting from the direction of Chihuahua's lodge and assumed the council must be under way. From the sound of things, the chief had his work cut out for him. He finished the tasty stew, a tangy mix of deer meat, wild onions, and herbs.

He thought about how the Oteros had deceived him and vowed to pay them back. How, he didn't know. But as sure as the sun rose in the east and set in the west, he would do his damnedest to help the Apaches or die in the attempt. The very notion of selling people as slaves galled him to the core.

Nalin took the gourd bowls outside and washed them using water from a jug. She returned, stacked the implements in a corner, and proceeded to lay out a blanket. "Is there anything more I can do for you?'' she asked.

"No. You have already done enough. Thank you.''

She stood and took a step, then halted and sat back down. "There is something I would like to tell you. If you would rather I leave, I will do so.''

Fargo moved to the blanket and reclined on his side. His head was still sore and his body ached, but overall he felt much better. He had a decision to make, and he must do so soon. If he was going to light out, he had to do it within the next hour or two, before the council broke up. Knowing Indians as he did, he knew it would take them at least that long to reach a decision concerning his fate. In the meantime, chatting with Nalin would help pass the minutes. "Talk,'' he signed.

She appeared relieved at the invitation. Her next remark, actually a question, caught the big man completely off guard. "Have you ever been lonely?"

"Every now and then," Fargo allowed, wondering what she was getting at.

"I hate being lonely," Nalin signed emphatically. "And since I was brought back from the Comanches, I have been lonely all the time."

"You were with the Comanches?"

Nalin's features clouded. "Yes. Eight years ago I was captured by the Comanches. One of their warriors took me into his lodge and made me one of his wives. For seven years I lived with him, and all this time my brother was looking for me, leading our warriors on raids of Comanche territory every chance he could. Not until about a year ago did he find the village in which I was held and free me."

Fargo listened attentively, impressed by the brotherly devotion that had prompted Nana to wage such a long search. He gazed idly out the doorway and spied a lone warrior armed with a bow standing ten feet from the wickiup. A guard, no doubt. "I am glad your brother saved you," he signed.

Nalin's mouth screwed into a scowl. "So was I. My heart sang until we returned and I discovered the men of our tribe are not very interested in having as a bride a woman who was abused by their hated enemies the Comanches."

Even Indians could be bigoted, Fargo reflected, and waited for her to come to the point. A profound sadness lurked in her eyes. He could imagine the sheer hell she'd been through. To be a tribal outcast was one of the worst fates that could befall an Indian. He was about to offer his sympathy when a tall figure materialized in the entrance.

Nana entered briskly and came over to them. He addressed his sister, then looked at the Trailsman. His hands flew in sign language. "My cousin has sent me to tell you that the council goes badly. He does not believe he can convince our people to spare your life." He scowled and spat a single word that summed up the entire situation. "Mangus!"

Rising, Fargo chided himself. So he knew Indians, did he? So they would take an hour or more, would they? He looked out the door at the guard, who was gazing toward Chihuahua's lodge, calculating a means of getting past the warrior unseen.

"Because my cousin owes you his life, he is giving you a chance to save yours," Nana went on. "As I told you earlier, your guns and horse are at my lodge. If you can reach them, you will have a chance to save yourself."

Nalin moved closer to them. "But he will have a hard time eluding the others if they give chase. They know the plateau well. He does not."

"True," Nana said. "But there is nothing we can do about it. I was sent to warn him, that is all. Now I must go back to the council and help our cousin."

"I could lead him down the western ravine," Nalin proposed. "The others will expect him to take one of the shorter ways toward the valley, which would be either east or south."

"You would be wise to stay here," her brother signed. "If anyone should learn that you helped this white man, they would demand you be cast out from our village."

"I want to help him," Nalin persisted.

Fargo motioned at the warrior. "Tell your cousin I thank him for his help. Tell him we are now even. I will get away on my own."

The muscular Apache gave a curt nod. "Then go in peace. But know that if we ever meet again, I will kill you." Wheeling, he left as silently as he'd appeared.

"I can show you a safe way down from the plateau," Nalin stressed to the Trailsman.

"You should stay out of this," Fargo advised her. "Your brother has the right idea." Strolling to the entrance, he watched Nalin hasten to the council. The guard looked at him and hefted the bow. Darkness had claimed the land and stars sparkled in the sky. Few Apaches were abroad. The men were all likely at the council, the women and children snug in their wickiups. He pivoted and walked to the opposite side of the lodge. From where he now stood, he couldn't see the warrior with the bow.

"What are you doing?" Nalin inquired.

Fargo pointed at the entrance. "This does not concern you. Leave so you will not get into any trouble."

Frowning, Nalin turned on her heels and sashayed into the night.

The very next instant Fargo was crouched beside the wall,

his throwing knife in his right hand. He went to work on the grass and brush matting, cutting a large hole at ground level, being careful not to rustle the dry vegetation too loudly. If fate smiled on him he'd be able to reach Nana's lodge undetected. It all depended on whether a sentry had been posted to the east as well as the west.

Soon he had an opening large enough for him to crawl through. Dropping flat, he peeked out and surveyed the village. As near as he could tell there was no guard. He slid the throwing knife into his boot again and slowly eased from the wickiup. The breeze caressed his cheeks. Off to the southeast a dog barked. Somewhere a horse neighed.

Fargo snaked toward Nana's lodge, covering half the distance when a cough sounded to his left. Freezing, he spied a woman walking toward another wickiup, her arms laden with branches to be used as firewood. He waited until she vanished inside before resuming his beeline to the pinto. Thankfully, the Ovaro was still saddled.

No fire blazed in Nana's lodge. Fargo eased through the entrance and paused to get his bearings. Without a light finding his revolver and the rifle would be difficult. He probed along the wall, his fingers running lightly over the ground. All along the south wall and the east wall he went without success. Just when he was beginning to think Nana had lied to him, his left hand closed on cold metal.

Elated, he found both guns lying on a blanket. He swiftly slid the Colt into its holster, grabbed the Sharps, and rose to a crouch. Now all that remained was mounting the stallion and hightailing it before the Chiricahuas discovered he'd given them the slip.

Just then rowdy shouting shattered the tranquility of the village. Fargo hurried to the entrance and saw a cluster of warriors heading toward the lodge where he'd been held. The council had already concluded! Walking at the head of the warriors, holding a torch aloft, was Mangus.

So much for using stealth. Fargo stepped to the Ovaro and untied the reins from the bush to which they'd been secured, trusting in the darkness to temporarily cloak his movements. He neglected to take into account, though, that Apaches were notorious night raiders; their night vision was keener than any white man's could ever be. As he swung onto the stallion a sharp cry burst from one of the warriors accompanying Mangus.

Fargo wheeled the pinto, cocking the Sharps as he did. The Apaches started toward him, Mangus in the lead. He took a hasty bead on the hateful cuss and fired, the big rifle booming like thunder. But at the very instant he did, another warrior darted in front of Mangus and took the lead meant for the stocky brave. As if flung by an invisible hand, the warrior was hurled back into the other Chiricahuas, throwing them into brief confusion.

Frowning, the Trailsman rode to the south, threading among the lodges, sliding the Sharps into its holster as he did. Yells broke out all over. Dogs barked furiously.

Fargo came to the southern edge of the village and galloped into the trees. Reining up, he glanced over his shoulder at dozens of torches flickering about. Soon the warriors would be after his hide. And, as Nalin had noted, they'd expect him to make to the east or south sides of the plateau. What if he did the opposite? If there was a ravine along the western rim, he felt confident he could find it and descend safely. Then he could swing a wide loop around the plateau and head for the valley.

He swung to the west, grateful there wasn't a full moon. The darkness would slow him down, but it would also make tracking impossible. Until daylight, at least, he'd have an edge over his pursuers. The village was in a total uproar. He heard horses riding to the south and grinned.

Unexpectedly, directly in front of him, a shadowy form astride a mount moved from behind a ponderosa pine.

Fargo's right hand instinctively closed on the Colt, bringing the revolver up for a snap shot. As his trigger finger began to tighten he saw long hair swaying and realized who it was. Peeved, he let her ride up beside the pinto, then jammed the .44 into its holster.

Nalin's white teeth flashed. She leaned toward him so he could see her arms move. "I decided to show you the way."

"Go back," Fargo signed. "I can find the ravine myself."

Instead of answering, Nalin turned around and headed westward.

He hesitated, aware he couldn't afford any delay and certainly couldn't spare the time to talk her out of being so stubborn.

Why was she doing this? Annoyed, he followed, his ears straining to catch the sound of warriors on their trail. They rode over a mile attended by normal night noises; the hoot of an owl, the distant howl of a coyote, and the rustling of underbrush as rabbits, polecats and such went elsewhere fast.

Nalin changed direction only once, cutting to the northwest, keeping to a rapid pace.

As another mile went by Fargo felt the tension drain from his body. He turned his thoughts to the Oteros, pondering a course of action. It would help matters if he knew what the Spaniard and his daughter were up to. Perhaps his best bet was to play along with them for a spell.

A line of large boulders appeared ahead. Nalin slanted to the right and moved between two of them.

Fargo elected to ride straight, passing between a different pair not six feet from the gap she'd used. Only when the Ovaro abruptly halted and shied violently did he realize he should have stayed on her tail. For there, not inches from the stallion's front legs, was a steep precipice with the bottom over a thousand feet below.

10

Fargo hauled on the reins in an effort to get the stallion to back away from the cliff rim. The pinto seldom displayed fear, but the unexpected sight of the drop off made it swing frantically to the right and left, seeking an avenue of escape. The boulders on either side prevented the Ovaro from turning. "There, there, big fella," Fargo said softly. "Take it easy." His voice soothed the horse and he guided it backward a good five yards.

Nalin was patiently waiting for him, a grin creasing her mouth. She moved her hands in exaggerated motions so he would catch every sign. "Are you in a hurry to reach the bottom?"

Slightly embarrassed by his close call, Fargo gave her a hard stare.

"I know another way," Nalin went on, not in the least intimidated. "It will take us longer and it is dangerous at night. If you would rather wait until morning I will understand."

"Lead the way," Fargo signed curtly.

Nalin turned her horse and went between the same pair of boulders she'd passed through previously.

This time Fargo stuck to her like maple syrup to a flapjack as she rode down a narrow incline that tapered into a trail barely wide enough for a full-grown horse to safely use. Neither of them could afford to use sign now. A single mistake would hurtle either of them to the rocks lurking at the base of the precipice, rocks ready to dash them to bits if they fell from such a great height.

The Ovaro didn't like the route one bit. He balked every now and then but continued downward at a word from his master.

Fargo was reminded of the ride across the narrow land bridge between the plateau and the rise earlier that day, only this was far worse. He scarcely breathed as they negotiated a serpentine path toward the bottom. Occasionally small stones would slide out from under the Ovaro's hooves and go clattering into the abyss. He never heard them hit.

The west wall of the plateau, it turned out, was the east wall of the broad ravine that extended for a good quarter of a mile. Towering stone walls were to the north and south, each several hundred yards away.

Fargo tried not to think of what would happen if, by a fluke, some of the Apaches found them and commenced firing from above. They would easily be picked off. He noticed that Nalin seemed unconcerned about the descent; she repeatedly looked at him and smiled encouragement or gazed serenely at the ravine walls. She was quite a remarkable woman and he wished there was something he could do to repay her kindness.

The harrowing ride down seemed to take the better part of the night. His nerves were jangled, his stomach muscles bunched in a tight knot. At last he saw the end of the trail. The stallion realized they were nearly down and tried to go faster, forcing him to draw on the reins before it knocked Nalin's horse over the side.

The Apache woman reached level ground and halted. She smiled at the big man as he stopped beside her. "My people seldom use that trail. Several have died trying. Even in the day it is very hazardous."

"I know I will never use it again," Fargo predicted. He stared at the mouth of the ravine. "It is a long ride back to the valley. I should be on my way."

"May your journey be safe."

Fargo nodded and went to ride off when a thought struck him. "What about you? What will you do?"

"Wait until morning and ride back up the way we came down," Nalin signed.

"All by yourself? What if you have an accident?" Fargo questioned, craning his neck to peer at the rim. He didn't want to leave her there alone, not after all she had done for him.

"Such things happen," Nalin said. "In daylight it should be much easier."

"I think you should ride with me to the south side of the plateau and get to the top the same way I did," Fargo proposed. "Why risk your life when it is not necessary?"

Nalin took a moment to reply. "Thank you for your concern. I will be fine," she said, and started to move forward.

"Stop," Fargo signed. He had an obligation to her and himself not to let her come to harm. And since leaving her to fend for herself until morning, even if she was an Apache, put her at great risk, he had but one choice. "I will stay with you until first light, then we will ride together around the plateau."

"This is not right. It will only slow you down."

"I can take my own sweet time returning to the valley," Fargo told her. "Your safety is more important." He didn't bother to add that he could use some rest and so could the stallion after its ordeal.

She bowed her head. "Whatever you want."

The big man took the lead, riding to the end of the ravine where the wind was strongest, a blast of cool air whipping out of the northwest. Turning due south, he found the land barren of trees and dotted with boulders. After traveling for five minutes he spied a bald hillock. To its west were several boulders the size of Conestogas arranged in a semicircle. He rode to the base of one and dismounted.

Nalin did likewise. She stretched, then suddenly grinned and pointed, uttering a single word in the Chiricahua tongue.

Fargo looked up and beheld a shooting star streaking across the firmament. Some Indians considered such a sighting a good omen. He ground-hitched the Ovaro and sat down with a pronounced sigh.

Stepping slowly, Nalin came over and stood in front of him. Her features were exquisitely lovely in the subdued light, the shadows tending to soften the contours of her face. "I will try to find wood for a fire if you wish," she offered.

Fargo surveyed the bleak terrain and chuckled. "You would be wasting your time. Just have a seat and we will wait until morning."

Obediently, Nalin sat down right beside him, her legs extended, the hem of her buckskin dress primly positioned well below her knees. She glanced sideways at him and nervously smiled. When next she moved her arms in sign language, she did so tentatively, as if afraid of being too forward or being rebuffed. "How will we keep warm?"

The big man regarded her closely. He couldn't make up his mind whether she was simply asking an honest question or making a subtle pass at him. Since there was only one way to find out, he slowly leaned toward her and planted a gentle kiss on her mouth, letting his lips linger. If she had in mind what he hoped she had in mind, he'd soon know.

Nalin's arms looped around his neck and drew him closer. She mashed her lips against his, seemingly starving for affection, and made a cooing sound deep in her throat. Her tongue touched his, exploring, seeking a taste of him.

Fargo responded ardently, inflamed by her passion. He ran his big hands over her buckskin dress, cupping her breasts and squeezing until she moaned. She pressed against him, her fingers running through his hair, causing his hat to fall off. Not that it mattered at the moment.

He rose to his knees, drawing her up with him, then reached his right hand down to probe under her dress. Her smooth legs and silken thighs made his organ throb. He stroked those thighs, up and down, feeling his blood pound and listened to her whimper.

If Nalin's passion was any indication, then she truly hadn't been with a man in ages. She couldn't get enough of him, her hands eagerly roving all over his body. Her right hand circled his groin, then pressed onto his member.

Aroused to a fever pitch, Fargo brought his right hand higher and cupped the hot mound between her legs. Her short hairs crinkled under his touch. He let his forefinger lightly touch her moist slit and she arched her back, grinding her hips and breasts against him.

He slowly inserted his fingers, feeling the slick walls of her tunnel close around them. She groaned, a wavering, drawn-out expression of her sexual hunger. When he began stroking her, she held him close and mouthed words in her language that he didn't understand.

Nalin suddenly bit him on the neck, then grabbed his shoulders and voiced a loud, "Uuuummmmm."

Using his left hand, Fargo hitched her dress well up on her hips. He curled his hand around her buttocks, feeling them twitch as her thighs quivered and her legs pressed against his other hand stimulating her inner core. He stroked forcefully.

"Aaaaah!" Nalin cried.

He eased her onto her back on the hard ground. Although his knees ached when he leaned down, he didn't give a damn. Keeping the fingers inside her, he hitched at his belt buckle and removed the gunbelt. Then came the buckskin pants, dropping around his knees. His maleness waved in front of her and she looked at it and gulped.

Fargo finally removed his fingers, and lowered the tip of himself into her slit. She cooed and squirmed, and then with a powerful thrust of his hips he drove inside her to his full length.

Nalin screamed.

The Trailsman commenced an in-and-out motion, flinching when she dug her nails into his back. She clung to him almost in desperation, matching her body's rhythm to his own, her buttocks rising to slap against his hips each time he thrust. He wanted to prolong the climax for as long as he could, to give her the greatest pleasure possible.

Moments later Nalin reached her peak. She bucked and thrashed under him, her head twisting from side to side, her mouth curled upward in either a grin of delight or a silent snarl. "Iieeee! Aaaaaah!"

He knew she was at the point of no return and he moved to meet her there, feeling an irresistible force building inside him that burst out his loins in an incredible explosion of pure ecstasy. He pumped and pumped, his body damp with perspiration, locking his lips on hers at the ultimate moment of their binding.

At last, spent, his rocking movement slackened and he lay still on top of her, breathing deeply, hearing her do the same. The sexual release, coming on the heels of his narrow escape from the village and the treacherous descent of the plateau, was doubly refreshing. She shifted and he realized his great frame might be hurting her. Accordingly, he rolled onto his side and stared into her grateful eyes.

Giggling, Nalin pecked him on the cheek and snuggled flush with his chest. She tenderly stroked his neck and chin, drinking in his rugged features with her gaze.

Fargo stared off into the distance, thinking of his return to the Otero *hacienda*. Somehow he must get to the bottom of whatever the hell the Oteros were up to. Why had the Spaniard and his daughter taken to killing the Apaches wholesale instead

77

of capturing more Chiricahuas to send south to the mines or wherever? He'd like to know before he put the Oteros out of business. And he would, too.

Not that the Apaches qualified as saints. Some bands were worse than others, and the Chiricahuas had a much deserved reputation for being as savage a bunch as any in the southwestern part of the United States. But the notion of slavery went against his grain. Putting folks in chains and dragging them hundreds of miles from their homes to spend the rest of their lives working at enforced hard labor was a practice almost too cruel to imagine.

He felt Nalin stir and glanced at her. She stood so she could arrange her dress down past her knees again and smooth her hair.

"I am grateful," she signed.

"That makes two of us," Fargo responded.

"It has been a long time. I had forgotten how wonderful the touch of a man can be."

The big man grinned. "I will be more than happy to remind you anytime you want."

Nalin laughed, truly at ease for the first time since they'd met. She abruptly stopped and swung to the north.

Fargo heard a faint noise, a peculiar series of loud cracks punctuated by a booming sound resembling distant thunder. He instantly shoved off the ground, pulling his pants up as he stood. Quickly retrieving the gunbelt, he buckled it on and loosened the .44 in its holster. "Did you hear that?" he signed.

"Yes," Nalin confirmed.

"What do you think it was?"

"Someone is descending the trail from the plateau. They must have accidentally dislodged a boulder."

"Then we were not as clever as we thought," Fargo commented. He stepped to the Ovaro, then faced her. "Mount up. We have some hard riding to do."

Nalin nodded and was mounted in no time.

Fargo had to hand it to the Chiricahuas; they didn't miss a trick. He figured some of the warriors had made a lucky guess, had decided to check the western rim just in case. But how in tarnation did the Apaches know he'd actually gone down that way? Had they used torches and found the Ovaro's tracks? He frowned, gripped the reins, and headed out.

On his left rode Nalin. Every now and then she looked at him, admiration etching her countenance.

The Trailsman reckoned he had an ample head start on any pursuers. Since the warriors couldn't track very fast, even if they were using torches, he'd be able to lose them without too much effort. Accordingly, he didn't push the pinto as hard as he might, and he'd covered less than half a mile when a new sound from their rear made him realize he'd gravely miscalculated. The Apaches weren't tracking him by themselves; they had help.

The excited barking of several dogs rent the night.

11

The very idea of Apaches using dogs to track someone shocked the Trailsman into reining up and surveying the murky landscape to their rear. He looked at Nalin, who had stopped when he did, and saw she wore a worried expression.

"Satanta!" she declared anxiously. "He has trained his dogs to hunt deer. I had no idea he could use them to hunt people too."

"Damn," Fargo swore in English, then changed to sign language. "Stay close to me. They will catch us in no time unless we ride to beat the wind." So saying, he spurred the stallion into a gallop, rankled at being outfoxed so handily. He'd known that Apaches were clever devils; now he knew just *how* devious they could be. Those dogs probably had the Ovaro's scent, not his, and wouldn't lose it unless he found water, a stream or a river he could take to and stick with for miles if need be to shake them. Of equal concern was the number of warriors with the dogs. If half the men in the village were along, he'd never get to make the Oteros pay for their misdeeds.

Taking the lead, the big man pushed southward for almost an hour until he came to the southern edge of the plateau. He cut to the left, making for the same rise from which he'd first viewed the tableland. Patches of vegetation appeared here and there, mainly creosote bushes and prickly pear cactus. He passed a few saguaro, the largest of all cactus plants, and an inspiration struck him.

Fargo waited until they neared more cactus plants, this time several of the barrel type, then hauled on the reins. He was down from the saddle before the stallion ceased moving. Taking the Arkansas toothpick from its sheath, he swiftly went to work slicing off strips of the outer skin, being very careful in the process not to let the sharp, nasty barbs pierce his flesh. He took the strips and placed them at random directly on top of the prints made by their horses, the barbed sides up. In the dark, he hoped, the dogs might not notice until it was too late.

Nalin watched in curious fascination as the man in buckskins positioned eight pieces of cactus. Comprehension dawned and she stared at him with heightened respect.

Satisfied with his handiwork, Fargo mounted and turned eastward. Occasionally he heard the dogs bark and guessed the mongrels must be three-quarters to a mile distant. When they reached the rise he went straight up, forced to bend forward over the pommel and clamp his legs onto the pinto's sides to keep from sliding backward. Nalin stayed right behind him.

At the top they paused to let the horses catch their wind. To the west arose more barking, the volume indicating the dogs were much closer.

Fargo was about to head down the opposite slope when a frenzied chorus of agonized howls and yelps signified that the mongrels had stumbled on the cactus strips. He pictured them prancing about in agony or thrashing on their sides, their paws lanced with slender spikes, unable to support their own weight. The Apaches would not be able to resume their pursuit until the barbs were extracted.

Nalin grinned, then moved her horse closer and signed, "This is where I must leave you." She pointed at the land bridge linking the rise to the plateau. "I must return to our village and check on my brother and Chihuahua."

"It is too dangerous to go across now," Fargo advised her. "Wait until dawn."

"I will be fine," Nalin replied. "My horse is surefooted and I have crossed over many times."

Fargo still didn't like to see her go. "What about the others in your village? Will they blame you for my escape and punish you?"

"I doubt anyone has noticed I am gone," Nalin stated. "No one pays much attention to me. I can slip back into the village without being seen. At first light I will come out of my wickiup as if nothing out of the ordinary has happened."

He knew arguing would prove fruitless. Leaning over, he gave her a kiss, then sat and watched her as she traversed the narrow bridge. Once he saw her horse halt, tossing its head, and he stiffened, fearful she would plunge over the side. The animal kept going, though, and Nalin attained the safety of the plateau unharmed. She looked back so he waved.

Kneeing the stallion, Fargo rode to the bottom of the rise. With the Apaches to the west no longer a threat, he had to concern himself with search parties that had already passed over the bridge and were somewhere up ahead and with any warriors who had descended the east side of the plateau where another way down supposedly existed.

He was all caution for the better part of two hours. The tableland fell far behind and still he saw no sign of hostiles. Before long the first fingers of pink and red streaked the eastern horizon, reminding him that he had been up for pretty near twenty-four hours without rest. He felt it, too, in his weary muscles and sore legs. That soft bed at the *hacienda* beckoned invitingly.

Thinking of the bed brought the Oteros to mind and he scowled. They had played him for a fool, expecting him to do their dirty work for them and not become any the wiser. Which brought him back to the same old question: What *was* their dirty work? What were they up to?

By the time the top of the sun appeared, Fargo was winding among the foothills bordering the mountains. He could see the fertile valley and a thin spiral of smoke wafting skyward from the house, probably from the stove as the cook prepared the morning meal.

There were now trees on all sides. He found a narrow game trail and took it, knowing from experience that wild animals invariably picked the easiest path to wherever they were going. In this instance the trail led over a hill and toward a creek visible to the southeast.

A glint of sunlight off metal in the trees to Fargo's right galvanized him into instant action. After years of surviving in the wilds where lightning reflexes often meant the difference between life and death, he instinctively responded to peril the second he discerned it. In this case, so superbly coordinated were his alert mind and muscular body that the very instant he detected the glint of light, he grabbed the stock of the Sharps and hurled himself to the left, diving from the Ovaro and hauling the Sharps with him.

A rifle boomed in the woods and lead smacked into the ground inches from the pinto's legs. The stallion bolted.

Fargo wasted no time in sprinting to the nearest cover and dropping to his knees behind a tree. A second shot thudded into the trunk, causing chips to fly. He stayed put, composing himself, wondering who in the world was out there. The odds of it being the Apaches were remote; the Chiricahuas possessed few firearms and they probably didn't come this far in search of him. But if not them, then who?

He peeked out and saw no sign of anyone. Whoever it was would likely be moving to a different position so he concentrated on the shadows in the general vicinity of the spot where the sunlight had gleamed off the rifle motion. He cocked the Sharps and waited patiently, and soon he was rewarded by seeing a flicker of white against the backdrop of green. Snapping the stock to his shoulder, he took a hasty bead and squeezed the tigger.

A sharp cry greeted the booming retort.

Fargo didn't budge. Dashing headlong from concealment would invite a ball or bullet in the brain. If someone was so all-fired determined to kill him, let them come to him and give away their location. He reloaded, and while doing so strained his ears to catch any noise the bushwhacker might make. The muted snap of a twig rewarded his effort, but it came from *behind him.*

Spinning, Fargo scoured the woods. Perhaps an animal had been the culprit. Suddenly he spied someone off to the left, bent over at the waist, moving through the undergrowth and looking every which way, clearly hunting for him. He sighted the Sharps, waited until the figure stepped into a narrow opening in the vegetation, and fired.

The big rifle belched flame, smoke, and lead, and the ambusher was lifted from his feet to crash into a thicket, disappearing from view.

Since the second shot might enable his attackers to pinpoint his exact position, Fargo placed his right hand on the butt of the Colt, tensed his legs, and dashed deeper into the trees, hunching over to minimize the target he presented. No one took a shot at him and he reached the shelter of another trunk. Again he reloaded the Sharps.

Silence gripped the wilderness. Not so much as a bird chirped. The gunfire, as always, had cowed the mountain creatures into retreating into their dens and burrows or flying elsewhere.

Fargo leaned his left shoulder on the tree and scrutinized his surroundings. Until he knew for certain how many there were, he wasn't about to take any chances. That figure he'd shot had not been dressed like an Indian; more like a *vaquero*. Which gave him much food for thought as five minutes elasped, then ten.

He began to think there were no more. Fatigue gnawed at his mind, making him drowsy, and he had to repeatedly shake his head to keep fully alert. If he stayed there long enough he might well doze off. That thought prompted him to move stealthily forward toward the area where he'd downed the second ambusher. He anticipated the man might be long gone, wounded but still alive.

Fargo slowed as he neared the thicket. He spied a pair of boots and the bottom half of two legs jutting out. Halting, he glued his eyes to those feet, thinking they would move. A full minute went by before he took the risk to glide closer. At last he could see the man clearly, and he wasn't very surprised at what he found.

The lead had struck the man full in the chest, blowing out a hole the size of a fist. Blood seeped from the edge. The man's eyes were locked wide in shock and his right hand still clamped on the rifle he'd been carrying. His Mexican-style clothing left no doubt as to his identity. He could only be one of the *vaqueros* working for the Oteros.

Fargo had the nagging suspicion he should know the man from somewhere. He racked his memory to no avail. Then, taking the ambusher's rifle, he worked his way toward the game trail. To the east, perhaps fifty yards off, stood the Ovaro calmly munching on grass. Changing direction, he made for his horse.

A rifle cracked across the way.

To the Trailsman, it seemed as if an invisible knife slashed him across the right cheek, stinging terribly. He flattened, knowing he'd been creased, feeling blood trickle down his skin. Someone had his range. He used his elbows and knees to crawl into a patch of high weeds, then stopped to give another listen.

His attackers were most persistent. Evidently they intended to stick around until they put a slug in him or they were prime worm food.

Fargo speculated on who might have ordered the *vaqueros* to kill him. The Oteros? It made no sense. Celestino and Gitana had hired him to get a job done, and he doubted either one would want him planted six feet under until that job was done, especially since they were so keen on wiping out the Chiricahuas. And if not them, then one likely candidate remained: Reyes Feliz.

The man in black hated Fargo. Whether from professional jealousy, bigotry, or perhaps an interest Feliz might have in Gitana, the *pistolero* wanted him dead. Fargo believed that Feliz and several *vaqueros* had fired at him the other night from behind the trees in the yard. If so, this was their second try, and he was damned tired of having them take potshots at their convenience. He decided to take the fight to them.

Moving slowly, he crawled from the weeds, being careful not to let the vegetation sway and shake, and kept going for another fifteen yards until he attained the shelter of a boulder about four feet high. Rising to his knees, he worked his way to the left and peeked around the edge.

Someone was coming down the opposite slope.

Fargo spied a *vaquero*, and this one he recognized. It was the man who wore the white *sombrero,* the same one he'd seen talking to Feliz, one of those who had watched him ride out yesterday morning. Had Feliz posted them to watch for his return and kill him on sight? If so, how had they known the route he would take? Or had they been on top of one of the hills and spotted him from a distance? Not that it mattered, because this one was as good as dead.

He leaned the Sharps against the boulder and hefted the rifle he'd taken from the dead *vaquero*, an old Hall's smoothbore, short-barreled carbine. Using the boulder as a brace for the barrel, he took his sweet time aiming. The *vaquero* was moving furtively and keeping low, his gaze on the weeds where Fargo had gone to ground.

Keep coming, you son of a bitch! Fargo thought, and cocked the carbine. He wanted a head shot and the *vaquero* obligingly still wore the white sombrero, an ideal target if ever there was one. But the *vaquero* seldom stayed still long enough for a certain kill.

Soon the hand came to the last brush before the game trail. He rose to his elbows for a good look.

Fargo was ready. His finger curled around the trigger and the carbine blasted. He saw the *vaquero* flip onto his side. Dropping the carbine, Fargo drew the .44 and ran toward the ambusher, ready to cut loose if need be. But further gunplay was unnecessary. The *vaquero* had been hit in the left eye, the shot passing completely through his head to burst out the back of his skull. Beside him lay the sombrero, now stained with blood and bits of gore. The man's shirt had been torn high on the right shoulder and a small red smear indicated where he'd been creased earlier by Fargo's first shot.

Straightening, Fargo suddenly realized that he'd made a mistake in exposing himself without confirming if there were more *vaqueros* about. His fatigue was making him careless. In confirmation, from his rear, came the distinct click of a hammer being pulled back.

12

Fargo dodged to the right and whirled, going to one knee as he turned, the Colt leveled at his waist. Eighteen feet away beside a tree stood a third *vaquero*, a revolver in his right hand, and he snapped off two quick shots that missed. Fargo's didn't. He thumbed the hammer twice, the two shots sounding almost as one, and the *vaquero* danced backward, then collapsed on his back, his legs kicking, the revolver falling from his twitching fingers.

Rising, keeping the man covered, Fargo advanced until he stood over the bushwhacker. The man's eyes silently appealed to him for aid. A pair of holes in the *vaquero's* shirt, above the heart, showed that there was nothing Fargo could do even had he been so inclined, which he wasn't. "Why?" he asked, hoping to glean some information, and tried the question again in Spanish. "*Por que?*"

The *vaquero's* lips compressed, then quivered as if he was on the brink of answering. Instead of replying, though, he tried to spit on the Trailsman but his mouth was too dry and he couldn't gather the saliva he needed.

"I reckon I'll oblige you after all," Fargo said, and put the *vaquero* out of his misery with a shot between the eyes. He then reloaded the .44 while surveying the forest for additional ambushers.

Slowly the hills came to life again. Birds sang. A woodpecker tapped on a nearby tree. Ground squirrels scampered about.

Fargo retrieved the Sharps but left the carbine where it lay. For the time being he didn't want anyone at the *hacienda* to know he'd tangled with the trio so he wasn't going to take anything back that could be linked to them. The buzzards and other carrion eaters would dispose of the bodies in short order if the corpses weren't found. He certainly had no intention of burying them; bushwhackers hardly deserved a proper planting.

He walked to the Ovaro and mounted. Feeling more fatigued than he had in ages, he headed for the valley. The sun warmed his face and shoulders and he pressed eastward until he was riding along the road between large herds of cattle. He spied a few *vaqueros*, none of whom paid him more attention than a passing scrutiny.

Fargo felt relieved when he could plainly see the house. He wanted to get into bed and sleep for a month. The farm hands were abroad in the tilled fields, busy at work. When he came to the yard, he saw a horse tethered near the front steps. The animal was caked with sweat, its sides heaving, almost on its last legs. Someone had practically ridden it into the ground.

As he climbed down a servant materialized to take the pinto. He grabbed the Sharps and paused just long enough to issue instructions. "Make sure my horse is watered, fed, and rubbed down proper. Understand?"

"Si, senor," the man answered, smiling.

The big man took the steps two at a stride. At the top another servant opened the door. From down the hallway drifted the sound of Gitana Otero's voice, drawing him like a magnet to the sitting room where he found the firebrand and her father in earnest conversation with the very man who had hired him: Jose Rojos. The foreman's clothes were coated with dust.

Gitana looked up and spotted the Trailsman almost instantly. She beamed and ran over. "Skye! You're back! I was afraid the Apaches might get you."

"They tried," Fargo said, entering.

"Did you locate their village?" Gitana asked hopefully.

"No," Fargo lied. "But I came close. After I rest up I'll head out again. It shouldn't take long."

"Excellent," Gitana said happily, and translated for her father.

Rojos walked over to shake hands. "I am glad to see you again, Mr. Fargo," he said in his clipped English. "And I bring good news."

"It must be good," Fargo commented. "That horse outside is about to keel over."

"I wanted my *patron* to know as soon as possible," Rojos said excitedly, and chuckled. "You brought me luck, after all."

"I did?"

"Without a doubt. I have secured the services of six men who will help you drive the savages from our land. They have fought Indians many times and never been beaten."

Fargo noticed happy expressions on Celestino and his daughter. "Who did you get? The U.S. Army?"

"Not quite," Rojos said. "It was my fortune to run into these men at a *cantina*. They have ridden together for several years now and they have a reputation as being men who can get any job done."

"Do you plan to keep me in suspense all day?"

"No," Rojos responded, grinning. "The men I have hired are lead by Jesse Walker. Perhaps you have heard of him?"

Fargo could have been floored with a feather. Everyone in the Southwest knew of Jesse Walker, a hardcase if ever there was one; a former soldier who had been dishonorably discharged for participating in a massacre of innocent Cheyennes. After the army gave Walker the boot he began working as a scout for wagon trains. Next he had a brief spell as a town marshall in Kansas where, rumor had it, he dipped his fingers into the town treasury and the good citizens sent him packing on the next stage out. Other hardcases started riding with him, and they made a specialty out of working for ranchers who were having rustling problems. Walker and his boys handled such nuisances quietly and permanently.

Fargo had once spoken to an oldtimer in a saloon who claimed there was more to Walker and his bunch than met the eye. It was the oldtimer's opinion that the ranchers were being played for fools. He maintained that Walker's bunch was actually doing the rustling they would later be hired to eliminate. When Fargo had pressed the oldtimer for proof, the man had merely smiled and sipped more whiskey.

"You have heard of him, yes?" Rojos was saying.

"Who hasn't?" Fargo rejoined, hoping his worry didn't show. Walker's wild bunch shouldn't be taken lightly. Between them and Reyes Feliz and the *vaqueros*, the Chiricahuas might well be wiped out. He had to find out what the Oteros were up to and do it quickly.

"Isn't it marvelous?" Gitana asked, clapping her hands in delight. "After all this time our problems will be eliminated. Our valley will be safe."

89

"How soon will Walker get here?" Fargo interrupted.

"In three days," Rojos answered. "He had business to conclude in Tucson first. Mr. Walker said he was most eager to meet you after all he has heard about your exploits."

"You told him I was here?"

"I told him I had hired you," Rojos said. "Why? Is something wrong? Should I have kept it a secret?"

"No," Fargo said, sighing. "I reckon it doesn't make any difference."

Gitana stepped closer and studied him. "You seem upset. What's bothering you?"

"Nothing," Fargo replied testily. "It's just that I've been up for over twenty-four hours, riding hard most of the time, scouring the mountains for the Apaches, and I could really use some food and a good sleep."

"I should have realized," Gitana said, turning to the doorway. "Dolorita! Dolorita!"

The pretty maid hastened into the room. She listened attentively while her mistress issued directions, then she bowed and departed.

"My maid will bring a meal to your room shortly," Gitana stated. "I also ordered her to have your bath prepared. After all that riding you must want to get the dirt off your body."

Actually, a bath had been the last thing on Fargo's mind. But since Gitana was going to so much trouble on his account he saw no reason to decline. Besides, a hot bath would relax him nicely and make him sleep like a baby. "Thanks."

Celestino spoke for the first time, gesturing toward the rear of the house.

"My father reminds me that we must find Reyes and break the good news to him," Gitana related. "By nightfall all the *vaqueros* and our farm hands will know." She paused and grinned. "Maybe we should hold a party to celebrate."

"Celebrate what?" Fargo queried. "Walker isn't even here yet and the Apaches are still alive and kicking."

"But their days are numbered. I can feel it," Gitana stated confidently. She leaned forward, lowering her voice as if confiding in him. "And I use every excuse I can to throw a *fiesta*. Some of our *vaqueros* play the guitar wonderfully and

I love to dance. Please be sure to attend. It will be on the portico.''

"If I'm awake I'll come down," Fargo said, "but I'm not making any promises." He nodded at her father and the foreman, then wheeled and went upstairs to his room. Every muscle felt leaden. After propping the Sharps in a corner, he walked to the window and stared down to see the Oteros and Rojos heading for the bunkhouse.

How the blazes was he going to find out what they were up to in only three days? He considered asking around among the farm hands and *vaqueros*, then discarded the notion. In the first place he didn't speak fluent Spanish. In the second place, one of those he spoke to was bound to report it to the Oteros, landing him in hot water.

"*Senor* Fargo?"

The big man spun. Dolorita stood in the doorway bearing a tray of food. "*Gracias*. I'm so hungry I could eat a horse."

She came in and moved to the foot of the bed. Gently resting the tray on the quilt, she smiled at him and began to leave.

Fargo took a step toward her, then recalled how she had raced off the last time and froze. "Wait," he urged. "I want to talk to you."

"Not again, please," Dolorita said. "We have nothing to talk about."

"I think we do. At least you can tell me what has been going on around here."

"I don't understand."

"What do you know about the Chiricahuas?" Fargo asked bluntly, unprepared for the stark terror that popped into her eyes a second before she whirled and ran out even faster than she had the last time. "Damn," he muttered. He'd handled that badly. What if she informed Gitana? The risk, he figured, was slight. He got the feeling that Dolorita and Gitana weren't on the best of terms.

Crossing to the bed, he sat down and dug in with gusto. Filling his belly made him drowsy, and he was about to turn in when Dolorita returned with two servants, toting the hot water for his bath. He stayed on the bed and watched them, amused that the maid averted her face the entire time.

Once they were gone, Fargo closed the door and strolled to the bathroom. He tested the water with finger, then stripped off his gunbelt and his clothes. Uttering a grateful sigh, he sank into the tub and leaned back, letting the heat evaporate the tension from his body. He closed his eyes, his mind drifting, thinking of a fine lady he knew in Denver and how he was long overdue to pay her a visit. His chin bobbed onto his chest, and before he could stop himself he dozed off.

Fargo came awake with a start. He blinked, gazing at the bathroom, then grinned at his foolishness. If he wanted to sleep, the bed was a much better place than the tub. The water had cooled but still felt warm on his skin, indicating he'd slept for at least half an hour, maybe longer. Dipping both hands under the surface, he went to splash water on his face when he heard a faint creak to his rear, the sound a floorboard might make under someone's weight.

Twisting so abruptly he caused the water to splash over the side, Fargo saw no one in the bathroom. The door to the bedroom stood partially open and there was no sign of anyone in there. Chiding himself for having a bad case of nerves, Fargo faced forward, bent down, found the washcloth and soap Dolorita had left in the tub, and began to wash his face. He closed his eyes to prevent them from burning.

Distinct footsteps sounded from the direction of the bedroom, the patter of running feet.

Fargo opened his eyes and turned, rising as he did, the lather momentarily distorting his vision. But he saw well enough to see a burly *vaquero* hurtling toward him with a gleaming knife held in an upraised hand. Trapped in the tub, knowing the man would be on him before he could step out and grab the Colt, he blinked his eyes and braced for the attack, feeling supremely stupid at being caught in the altogether.

The *vaquero* hissed and swung.

The Trailsman barely got his hands up in time to catch the man's wrist and keep the blade from plunging into his chest. Driven against the front of the tub by his assailant's momentum, Fargo lost his balance. Somehow he managed to retain his slippery grip on the man's arm, and when he fell over the side he hauled the *vaquero* down with him. In the process he upended the tub.

There was a loud crash as Fargo landed on his right side, the *vaquero* on top, and suddenly they were both awash in his bath water. The man glared hatred in his eyes and they struggled furiously. Neither of them could get much of a purchase until the *vaquero* succeeded in rising to one knee. Fargo slugged him on the chin, smashing the man's teeth together, then drove his right fist into the *vaquero's* midsection.

Uttering a feral growl, the *vaquero* wrenched backward, jerking his wrist free, and frantically heaved upright.

Fargo pounced, surging to his feet and seizing the man's knife arm while simultaneously planting a right fist on the *vaquero's* jaw. The man stumbled toward the bedroom, his boots nearly sliding out from under him on the soaked floor. Fargo, unwilling to let go and unable to retain his balance, also tottered. Together they fell through the doorway onto the carpet.

The *vaquero* tore himself loose and scrambled to his feet.

Rolling to the left to give himself some room, Fargo emulated his foe. He crouched and glanced at the Sharps in the corner beyond the bravo. It might as well be on the moon.

"Gringo!" the man snarled, and closed in, swinging the knife in wide arcs, trying to slash the Trailsman open.

Fargo was forced to retreat toward the wall, narrowly evading each strike, his fatigue entirely forgotten in the rush of the moment. The *vaquero* abruptly changed his tactics and whipped the knife up as if about to throw it. Shifting to the left, Fargo brought both arms in front of his body to ward off the blade. But the man vented a brittle laugh and resumed slashing. The bastard was playing with him, Fargo realized, and wished he could get his hands on the *vaquero's* throat.

Suddenly Fargo bumped into the wall, or he thought it was the wall until he felt soft material rubbing against his naked back. The curtains! He had inadvertently backed right up against the window. No sooner had he reached that conclusion than the *vaquero* bunched his shoulders, extended his knife arm, and charged like an enraged bull, attempting to gore him with the glittering blade.

13

At the very instant that the cutthroat charged, an ear-piercing, terrified scream arose from the doorway.

Fargo didn't take his eyes off the *vaquero*. He swiftly stepped to the right, the knife coming within a hair of cutting deep into his arms, and flicked his left foot out. His instep caught the man's left ankle, tripping the *vaquero*, making him pitch forward. Fargo added to the impetus by locking both hands together in a single fist and swinging his arms in a vicious circle, clipping his attacker on the back of the head.

The *vaquero* couldn't stop if he wanted to, and he very much wanted to. He screamed when his head plowed into the window, shattering the glass into hundreds of shards, and his feet left the floor. In a sparkling shower of fragments he sailed out and down, his arms swinging wildly as gravity took over and speedily brought him smashing onto the hard ground, face first.

A breeze stirred the curtains as Fargo moved over and stared down at the crumpled form. Blood already ringed the man's head. The knife lay nearby. He glanced toward the bunkhouse and saw the Oteros, Rojos, and Feliz at the southeast corner. Three of them were gaping in astonishment at the dead man. Feliz, however, merely glared at the broken window.

"Madre de Dios!"

The exclamation brought Fargo around to find Dolorita standing in the doorway, her hands clasped to her bosom. She gulped, her eyes straying lower to a point above his thighs.

"Oh, my," she said softly.

"Excuse me," Fargo said, and hastened into the bathroom. He rapidly dried himself with a towel, his temper flaring. Now that he had a moment to think, he was incensed that the *vaquero* had jumped him at the most vulnerable of moments and in the most private of places. There was no doubt who had put the man up to it; Reyes Feliz didn't miss a trick. The man in black deserved a bullet in the head and Fargo was going to be the one to do the job. He dressed quickly, strapped the Colt around his waist, and stalked out, hardly noticing the maid as she moved aside.

He went down the corridor to the top of the stairs, seeing red every step of the way. Then he paused, regaining his self-control, aware he was on the verge of making a big mistake. He couldn't prove Feliz had sent the *vaquero*, and if he gunned the man down the Oteros might decide to send him packing. Above all else, he didn't want to leave until he found out what the Spaniard and his daughter were up to.

Excited voices filled the lower floor and Gitana appeared on the run. Behind her were Feliz, the foreman, and her father. She started up the steps before she spotted the big man, then looked at the landing and halted in surprise.

"Skye! Are you all right? What happened? We saw one of our hands go flying out the window."

"Did you, now?" Fargo said sarcastically, hooking his thumbs in his belt. He strolled toward her, doing his level best to keep his anger in check, his eyes darting to Feliz who stood at the bottom wearing an uncertain expression. Thinking of Nalin, Nana, and Chihuahua helped; he owed them his life and meant to repay the favor.

"It was Carlos," Gitana said. "He's dead."

"I hope so," Fargo stated, stopping. "The man tried to kill me."

Gitana appeared confused. "I don't understand. Carlos has worked for us for over seven years and never given us any trouble. Why would he do such a thing?"

"You tell me."

Celestino spoke and Gitana turned, apparently launching into an extended explanation. Rojos chimed in but Feliz did not. Their conversation became heated with repeated gesturing at the Trailsman. Finally Gitana faced him again.

"This is all very strange. None of us have any idea why Carlos would try to take your life. Did he say anything that would give us a clue?"

"No," Fargo said. "He was too busy trying to stick his knife in me."

"I am happy he didn't," Gitana said with evident sincerity. "When I first heard the window break and glanced around, for a second I thought it was you falling out. My heart almost stopped beating."

Fargo didn't know whether to believe her feelings for him were genuine or not. Regardless, he had to make Feliz think that he distrusted all of them. "It seems that someone here wants me dead, and until I find out who it is I'm not going to turn my back on any of you."

"Surely you don't think my father or I had anything to do with this?" Gitana asked in surprise.

"I don't know."

"Think for a minute. Why would we have you killed when we need you to find the Apaches for us?"

Amused that he'd had the same thought himself, Fargo kept a straight face and said, "All I know is that one of *your* men attempted to stab me in *your* house. I should ride out of here right this minute. It would serve you right if the Apaches burn this place to the ground."

Gitana frowned, then relayed the news to her father. He responded and she faced the big man. "Although my *padre* had nothing to do with the attempt on your life, he apologizes for it. He begs you to stay on. And he promises to keep guards outside your door from now on."

"I can take care of myself," Fargo said. "From now on I'll prop chairs against the doors and if anyone tries to come in without knocking they'll be greeted with lead."

"Then you'll stay?" Gitana asked eagerly.

"For the time being."

"Good," Gitana said, beaming. She passed on the information to Celestino, who smiled and nodded at the Trailsman.

"For now I'm going to get some sleep," Fargo informed her. "And be damn sure that no one disturbs me until I wake up."

"Since you won't let me post men outside your room, I'll instruct two *vaqueros* to stand guard at the foot of the stairs," Gitana proposed. "No one will be able to go up or down without being seen. You will be completely safe."

"No one is ever completely safe," Fargo replied, and pivoted. "We all meet our Maker sooner or later, and when our time comes there isn't a thing we can do about it."

Gitana tried to inject some humor into their discussion by grinning and saying, "I had no idea you are such a philosopher."

"I'm not," Fargo said. "Just realistic." He headed back for his room, pleased with his performance. As far as Feliz knew, he didn't suspect him. Which meant the man in black might hang himself if Fargo gave him enough rope. He reached the doorway and stopped in surprise just outside. The maid was still there.

Dolorita was pacing nervously back and forth. She glanced up and halted. "Why did Carlos try to killing you?" she inquired in her imperfect English.

"I'd like to know the same thing," Fargo declared. "Do you have any ideas?"

She shook her head, then said almost in a whisper, "Did you know that Carlos and Reyez Feliz were the most best of friends?"

"No. Why? What difference does it make?"

"Carlos does what Feliz wants. Always."

"Are you telling me that Feliz put Carlos up to killing me? Why would he do a thing like that?"

Opening her mouth as if to reply, Dolorita abruptly changed her mind, shook her head, and hastened into the corridor. "I have said too much already," she said in passing.

The big man let her go. Sooner or later she might break down and confide everything she knew, but she wouldn't if he pressed her. Sometimes women had to be handled like horses; trying to ride them into submission only made them buck the harder. As many an experienced rancher knew, a little sugar often brought better results than too much whipping.

He stepped into the room and closed the door. Then he took a chair from the corner, wedging it tight under the latch so that anyone who wanted to enter would need to break the door down. He repeated the precaution at the door connected to the other bedroom.

Satisfied he was temporarily safe, Fargo stretched out on his back on the bed, keeping his Colt strapped around his waist. He tilted his hat down over his forehead, closed his eyes, and was soon asleep.

* * *

When he rejoined the world of the living, darkness shrouded the room. He glanced at the broken window as he sat up and saw the curtains swaying in a sluggish breeze. Evening had descended. From outside came the pleasant strains of guitar music. A man was singing in Spanish. Light laughter wafted up from below.

The *fiesta* must be in full swing, Fargo deduced, and stood. He stretched languidly, getting the stiffness out of his muscles and the kinks out of his joints. His stomach rumbled, letting him know he needed food.

He crossed to the door, shoved the chair out of the way, and went downstairs. Every light in the house was lit. Several servants were going from the kitchen to the back porch or in the opposite direction. He walked down the hall and paused at the back door.

The *vaqueros* and farm hands were mingling on the grass near the portico, the majority holding drinks. On the south side of the porch stood the six *vaqueros* who comprised the band. Four had guitars, one held gourd rattles, and the last man, of all things, a flute.

Celestino Otero and Jose Rojos sat at a table, clapping their hands in time to the music and watching a couple who were dancing a fandango: Gitana and Reyes Feliz.

Fargo stepped outside. He noticed the way Gitana and Feliz had eyes only for each other. The look on the *pistolero's* face, the devotion etched there, was added confirmation of his suspicion. Feliz was trying to have him killed out of pure jealousy.

He ambled over to the table and nodded at the father and the foreman. A few of the hands and *vaqueros* spied him and began whispering, no doubt discussing the death of Carlos. He ignored them and waited for the dance to finish. When everyone applauded, he joined in.

Gitana curtsied to Feliz, then turned and saw the Trailsman. "Skye!" she declared happily, and came over to take his arm. "Will you dance the next fandango with me?"

"I'm out of practice," Fargo said. "Reyes in doing fine. Keep dancing with him."

"But I want to dance with you," Gitana persisted, pouting.

"I'd probably break your toes."

"I'm serious."

"So am I."

Tugging on his arm, Gitana tried to lead him toward the dance area. "Come on, coward. When I want to dance with a man, he does it whether he wants to or not."

"Not this time," Fargo said flatly. "I just woke up and I'm in no mood to dance. Besides, I'm practically starved. Any chance of getting something to eat?"

"Will you dance once your belly is full?"

"We'll see."

Gitana pulled out a chair and motioned for him to sit. Then she turned and issued instructions to a nearby servant. The man promptly hastened into the house. "Your meal will be here shortly, *Senor* Fargo."

"I'm obliged."

"And I hope you choke on it," Gitana said, grinning impishly. She swirled over to Feliz, who hadn't budged since spotting the Trailsman. His hand hovered near his revolver, his fingers twitching, his hatred obvious to anyone with eyes to see.

But Fargo appeared to pay no attention whatsoever to the man in black. If Feliz prodded him, well and good. But otherwise he would let bygones be bygones until he discovered the Oteros' secret. He surveyed the yard and the buildings beyond, watching Feliz out of the corner of his eyes, and was grateful when the band broke into another song and Gitana prompted Feliz into dancing.

Soon Dolorita came outside carrying a plate of food and silverware. She deposited both on the table in front of him, then glanced around to be sure no one was paying much attention to them. As she straightened her lips brushed his ear. "I want to talk much later."

Fargo gave a barely perceptible nod and picked up his knife and fork. He deliberately didn't look at her as she went back into the house in case others might be watching. Inwardly he was excited that he might finally learn something substantial. The good news invigorated him and increased his appetite. He dug in, eating every last bit of the meal.

Across the table Celestino and Rojos conversed quietly in

Spanish. They studiously avoided looking at him, as if afraid of giving offense.

Gitana and Feliz danced several more numbers. They were encouraged by the applause of the *vaqueros* and the farm hands, many of whom were dancing themselves. Gitana, in particular, relished the attention, her face flushed with excitement as her supple body whirled and swayed.

Fargo finished and pushed his plate back. He saw several of the women who had been breaking their backs in the fields all day now spinning in delighted abandon and marveled that they found the energy. Idly gazing at the house, he spied Dolorita watching him from a downstairs window. She immediately disappeared.

Rojos leaned across the table. "I hope you are no longer mad at us," he said.

"Not in the least."

The foreman gestured toward the band. "Should I tell Gitana you are ready to dance?"

"Not if you like breathing," Fargo said, smiling, and Rojos burst into laughter.

Suddenly, from out of the night, bringing the music to an abrupt stop and freezing everyone in their places, came a chilling chorus of Apache war cries.

14

Fargo surged out of the chair, his right hand swooping to his Colt and clearing leather, as the thunder of hooves heralded the arrival of the raiders. Chiricahuas materialized out of the darkness, rounding the stable and the bunkhouse and flowing across the yard in a tight loop, loosing arrows and hurling lances at the astonished *vaqueros* and farm hands. Many fell, some screaming.

Panic ensued. The workers tried to break in every direction, bumping into one another in their haste, creating a logjam of cursing, shoving humanity. A few had the presence of mind to bring their guns to bear and shots boomed right and left.

Skye started to move toward Gitana, thinking he would protect her, but Reyes Feliz already had the chore well in hand. The man in black stood between the lawn and her, shielding her with his own body, his Dragoon belching smoke and lead.

An arrow streaked through the cool air, almost hitting Fargo's hat, and he ducked down next to the table and frowned. Here he was caught in the middle. By all rights his loyalties should be with the Oteros and their hired help since he was working for Celestino, but since he knew about the slaver operation the Otero family had conducted for decades, his sympathies were with the Apaches.

A *vaquero*, struck by a spear, screamed and fell.

A woman foolishly fled toward the stables and was cut down in midstride.

Fargo would have been content to keep low until the raid was over. Then he spotted the stocky form of Mangus at the head of the war party and rose, staying bent over at the waist as he cautiously moved toward the west edge of the porch. He raised the .44, aiming carefully, wanting to be sure, but several other Apaches rode in front of Mangus, blocking his view. Annoyed, he went farther, seeing a farm hand go down with an arrow between the shoulder blades.

Without warning a lone Chiricahua broke through the confused ranks of *fiesta* goers and made straight for the portico, a bow clutched in his right hand. He whooped and aimed at Reyes Feliz, who was preoccupied with another warrior.

It galled Fargo to save Feliz's life. But he knew that Apache bows were incredibly powerful, knew the shaft might well pass completely through the *pistolero's* chest and hit Gitana. Reluctantly he thumbed the hammer twice, the big Colt booming and bucking in his hand.

The bowman was knocked off his mount into the milling *hacienda* hands.

At the north end of the yard the Apaches were swinging about for another pass, Mangus at the forefront waving a lance and urging them on. In the flickering light from the lanterns ringing the porch the warriors were little more than shadowy wraiths whose indistinct features lent them the aspect of vengeful ghosts.

Most of the *vaqueros* had recovered from the initial shock and were putting up quite a fight. In their excitement and haste most missed. The constant gunshots filled the night with acrid smoke.

The Trailsman reached the grass and skirted a woman on her knees praying to the Almighty for deliverance. He saw Mangus begin the next charge, the entire band making straight toward the *portico*. Straightening and extending his right arm, Fargo sighted as best he could in the dim light, cocked the hammer, let the stocky killer ride a dozen feet nearer, and squeezed the trigger.

As if smacked in the forehead by a hammer, Mangus flipped end over end off his horse and under the hooves of those of his companions. The rest of the Chiricahuas kept coming, shooting arrows as rapidly as they could nock their bows.

Not three feet to Fargo's left a farm hand spun around and dropped with a shaft through his thin neck. Fargo shot the warrior who had done the deed, then pivoted and selected yet another target. Engrossed in aiming and believing that the only enemies he had to worry about at that moment were the Apaches, he was unprepared for the sudden stinging sensation in his left arm as a bullet struck him from behind just a few inches below the shoulder, causing a flesh wound that racked him with pain.

Twisting, Fargo dropped to his knees and stared at the porch. He figured Feliz had shot him, but there was no sign of the man in black or Gitana. Thundering hooves reminded him the war party was bearing down and that he was exposed and vulnerable out there in the open. He hurled himself toward the porch, rolling onto his back, and there were the foremost Apaches not a dozen yards distant. Sympathies or not, he wasn't about to be shot or trampled. The .44 cracked twice and two warriors fell.

A second later the war party veered away from the house and galloped toward the gap between the stable and the bunkhouse. A few stray shafts were fired but none scored. In moments the Apaches were out of sight, heading due west.

Several *vaqueros* foolishly continued to shoot, but their guns fell silent after half a minute. A foglike shroud of smoke hung above the grass. Bodies were everywhere, the majority Otero workers, some moving feebly or convulsing in the throes of death. Groans and pleas for help issued from a score of throats. Spreading pools of blood marked those who were dying.

Pressing the back of his right hand to his left shoulder, Fargo stood and grimly surveyed the lawn. Those who hadn't been hurt were going to the assistance of those who had. He stepped onto the porch, under a lantern, to examine his wound. A nasty furrow a quarter of an inch deep was bleeding into his sleeve.

"Mr. Fargo?"

The big man looked up. Kneeling near the table was Jose Rojos, his face a pale mask. And lying on his back next to the foreman, a feathered shaft sprouting from his chest, was Celestino Otero.

Fargo walked over. "Is he—?"

"Dead," Rojos said before the question was completed. He bowed his head and gently touched his patron's forehead. "I tried to get him to go inside but he refused and kept yelling for a gun. He was a fighter to the last."

And that's not all, Fargo reflected. He gazed at the other

bodies on the porch, one of them a guitarist who had been struck by a spear while holding his instrument in front of his chest. Now the guitar was pinned to the man's body.

"*Padre!*"

The piercing shriek brought Fargo around to see Gitana Otero dashing from the back door to her father's body. She wailed as she threw herself on top of Celestino and clasped him tightly. Great, soul-wrenching sobs racked her and she wept uncontrollably.

Reyez Feliz walked from the house, reloading the Dragoon, his sad eyes riveted on Gitana. Servants, farm hands, and *vaqueros* began to gather around. They all appeared to be in a state of shock.

Fargo stared at the man in black, uncertain whether Feliz had shot him or not. In all the commotion a wild shot could have been responsible, but somehow he doubted it. Call it intuition, call it a logical hunch, but he suspected that he would be dead if Feliz had been able to see a bit more clearly. Whatever the case, now was hardly the right time to press the issue. He slid the Colt into its holster and walked unnoticed into the house.

Coming toward him was Dolorita. She took one look at his arm and halted. "Come with me. I will dress up your wound."

Fargo didn't bother to correct her English. She led him to a small room off the main hall and advised him to wait, then hastened away. A rocking chair in one corner enticed the big man to sit down with a sigh and lean his head back. What would happen now that Celestino was dead? Would Gitana run the vast estate by herself? Or would she sell out and head for Mexico or Spain? He hoped it would be the latter. Once the ranch folded, the Apaches would no longer have to live in constant fear of being captured and sold into a life of miserable slavery.

Dolorita returned bearing a bowl of water and a cloth. She placed both on a small table near the rocking chair and applied herself to dabbing at the wound. "Does this hurt, *senor*?"

"No," Fargo said.

"I hear much crying," Dolorita commented.

"It's Gitana. Her father is dead."

"No!"

"Afraid so."

The maid stopped to listen to the sorrowful wailing. "I did

104

not know. This is a bad, bad night. The Apaches get much bolder each time.''

"Which reminds me. What did you want to talk about?"

Dolorita stiffened and glanced at the doorway, then leaned over him and lowered her voice. "Not so loud, *senor*. No one must hear or I am in big trouble, *si*?"

"I understand."

She placed the cloth in the bowl and began wringing it out, turning the water crimson. "You wanted to talk about the Indians, remember? At first I did not trust you. Now I know that you are in danger here, that some here think you might turn against the Oteros."

This was news to Fargo. "Who?" he asked, sitting up.

"I cannot say," Dolorita said. "But I heard words spoken when I should not have heard them. It is enough." She stepped up to him and pressed the cloth over the wound.

"What can you tell me about the Apaches?"

Her answer was whispered. "Many have been sold and sent to Mexico to work in mines. The Oteros have been doing this for more years than anyone knows. They have grown rich off the trade, not from cattle as they would have outsiders believe. Oh, they sell some cows, but most are used for food here."

"Why was a trap set for the Apaches the other day at the pass?"

"You know about that?"

Fargo nodded.

"Gitana hoped to wipe most of the Chiricahuas out. She set the trap. She sprung it."

"But why exterminate them?"

"Because of the investigation—" Dolorita began, then clammed up at the sound of footsteps.

Jose Rojos materialized in the doorway. "Mr. Fargo! There you are." He walked up to the rocking chair. "How badly are you hurt?"

"I'll live."

"Good. Feliz is organizing a party to go after the damn Chiricahuas. Would you care to go along?"

Fargo snorted. "Only a fool tries to catch Apaches at night. Anyone who goes with Feliz is just asking to be scalped. Wait until morning when their tracks can be seen."

"We plan to take torches."

"Which means the Apaches will see you coming miles away. You might ride into an ambush and every last one of you could be wiped out."

"Nevertheless we are determined to go," Rojos persisted. "Our beloved *patron* has been killed. We must avenge him."

"Is Gitana going along?"

"No. She is too distraught. Some of the hands are carrying Celestino's body inside even as we speak. I've advised her to go to her room. Two of the women will be with her at all times," Rojos said, and looked at Dolorita. "You should join them as soon as Mr. Fargo's arm is taken care of."

"*Si.*"

"If you want to get yourself killed, go right ahead," Fargo said. "I'm staying put until morning, then I'll try to track the Apaches. You'd be wise to tell your men to wait until then."

"We cannot wait," the foreman said stiffly. He turned on his heels and departed.

Fargo stared at the maid. "Now what was that business about an investigation? Who's doing the investigating?"

"Later, *senor*," Dolorita said, scooping up the bowl. "I must go to Gitana. If you want, I will bring medicine for your arm later."

"For this little scratch? Forget the medicine and tell me about the investigation."

"I'm sorry," Dolorita said, and rushed out as if her skirt was on fire.

Thwarted again, Fargo slumped in the chair and moodily contemplated his next move. The raid had taken him by surprise. He hadn't anticipated the Apaches would launch an all-out attack and wondered if he had inadvertently caused it. Maybe the Chiricahuas were thirsting for revenge because he had killed those three warriors near the spring and the other man in their village. Mangus would have been just the type to work the rest of the tribe into a fighting frenzy over the deaths. And since he hadn't seen any sign of Nana, he assumed the hotheaded Mangus had been leading the raid.

He heard loud crying and hushed voices as people came in the back door. A group of farm hands bearing Celestino's body walked past, then a cluster of women. Among them was Gitana, sobbing piteously.

Fargo saw her gaze absently into the room and halt at the sight of him. She clenched her fists at her sides and came up to the chair, doing her best to stop the tears from flowing.

"Did you see?" Gitana asked, a tremor in her voice. "Did you see those savages murder my father and butcher our people?"

"I saw," Fargo said.

"They are devils from hell! I will personally exterminate every last one of them!" Gitana vowed, her eyes blazing, her features flushed with fury.

"Maybe you should leave well enough alone."

Gitana recoiled in shock at the suggestion. "Leave those vile savages alone? Never! From now on I will be as ruthless as they are. I'll hire a hundred men, if necessary. I'll spend every last *peso* I own. And sooner or later I will have the satisfaction of seeing the last of the Chiricahuas skinned alive and left for the buzzards." She started to turn, then stared into the big man's eyes. "I'm surprised you would even make such a suggestion, Skye. Whose side are you on?"

Before Fargo could answer she spun and hurried into the corridor. He gloomily watched her leave. Any hope he might have entertained that Celestino's death would work out for the better was now gone. Knowing the firebrand as he did, he suspected that the real trouble was just beginning.

15

The sun hung above the eastern horizon when Fargo ventured downstairs the next morning after a fitful night of rest. In his right hand was the Sharps. The servants were up and about but not Gitana. He took his breakfast on the portico and ate sullenly.

All of the bodies had been removed shortly after the battle. The puddles of blood in the yard and on the porch had been cleaned up. Except for the front half of a broken Apache arrow lying in the grass there was no indication that the fight had even transpired.

Fargo saw farm hands going into the fields and a few *vaqueros* on their way to tend the cattle. Everyone wore a melancholy expression; a pall of death had gripped the *hacienda*. He pushed back his plate of eggs after eating a small portion and headed for the stable to retrieve the Ovaro. When almost there, he stopped at hearing the drumming of many hooves approaching from the west.

Into view came the search party, Rojos and Feliz in the lead. All the hands were covered with dust and appeared weary to the bone. A half-dozen or more were leading horses over which were slumped the lifeless forms of hapless companions. Quite a number had sustained injuries and wore makeshift bandages or were being assisted by their fellows. Rojos and Feliz led them toward the stable.

Halting, Fargo cradled the Sharps. "Howdy," he said when they were close enough.

"*Buenos dias,*" Rojos greeted him.

Feliz let his narrowed eyes do his talking.

"You were right, Fargo," Rojos went on as he reined up. "The Apaches saw us coming from far away. They set up an ambush in the mountains, in a narrow ravine, and opened fire when all of us were inside it. We were fortunate that any of us came out alive."

"I tried to warn you," Fargo reminded him.

"Yes, you did," Rojos said, dismounting. "In the passion of the moment, though, none of us was thinking clearly. The next time we won't be so careless."

The rest of the *vaqueros* began climbing down. All except the man in black. Feliz looked down at the Trailsman and scowled, his right hand draped on his leg near the Dragoon. "Did you have a good night's sleep, *hombre*?"

"Better than you did," Fargo retorted.

"And where are you off to now?"

"Not that it's any of your business, but I'm going to find the Apache village," Fargo fibbed. He had no intention of revealing its location to anyone in the valley.

"Perhaps you should take two or three *vaqueros* along," Fèliz suggested. "A lone man will have little chance to survive out there with the Indians so riled."

"I like to work alone."

Rojos, in the act of flipping a strirrup onto the saddle so he could undo the cinch, paused. "Reyes is right. The risk would be too great if you go out alone."

"I can manage," Fargo insisted.

"No doubt you can," Rojos said. "But since I was the one who hired you for my *patron*, I feel responsible for your safety until the job is done. I must insist that you take at least two men with you."

Fargo gazed at the house to prevent them from noticing the anger he felt. The last thing he wanted to do was have a couple of *vaqueros* trailing him all over creation. But if he refused, he might arouse suspicion. Rojos was already put out at him for not going along last night and Gitana had questioned his loyalty. If he wanted to stay on and find a way of helping the Chiricahuas, he had to play along for now. "All right. Pick two men."

"It will have to be two who didn't go with us last night," Rojos said, moving off. "They must be fresh, ready for a hard day's work. I will be back in five minutes."

Hefting the Sharps, Fargo entered the stable and soon had his saddle on the stallion and the rifle in its holster. Swinging up, he rode outside.

The foreman was approaching on foot. Behind Rojos were

two mounted *vaqueros*, both young men in their twenties.

"Here are two good men," Rojos said, and indicated each with a bob of his head. "Pedro and Felipe."

Pedro was the leaner of the pair, a wisp of a man wearing a brown sombrero and a revolver on his right hip, butt forward. Felipe wore a black hat and a green poncho that effectively hid any belt gun. Neither man seemed overjoyed at the prospect of accompanying the Trailsman into the mountains.

Fargo nodded at each one and touched his spurs to the Ovaro, heading around the stable and making toward the excuse for a road that bisected the ranch. He decided he would lead the two men on a wild goose chase, take the better part of the day to cover the mountains to the southwest, far from where the village lay.

The two *vaqueros* caught up with the big man, one riding on each side.

"Excuse me, please, *senor,*" Pedro said, his English heavily accented.

"What is it?" Fargo responded.

"I thought you should know that Felipe and I have not fought many Indians. We hired on here to work with cattle, nothing more. The *patron* did not tell us the Apaches would give us so much trouble."

Fargo had to admire the man's honesty. "Thanks for telling me. If it'll make you feel any better, I don't aim to get us killed if I can help it."

"*Si.* Thank you. It does make me feel better," Pedro said, and translated for his friend.

They took the same route Fargo had taken before until they came to the foothills, at which point Fargo turned to the southwest to carry out his plan. He stuck to the open country, avoiding forested tracts and narrow passes to preclude being ambushed again. There might be roving bands of Chiricahuas abroad and he didn't want to tangle with one.

The morning passed uneventfully. They saw deer, rabbit, chipmunks, and squirrels. At midday they halted beside a stream bordered by a cliff on the south and a meadow on the north. After letting the animals slake their thirst the men did the same.

Fargo sat at the edge of the bank and chewed on a piece of

jerked beef. The *vaqueros* sat a few feet away, whispering in Spanish. Finally Pedro looked at him.

"Would you shoot us in the back, *senor*?"

Surprised, Fargo glanced at them and lowered the jerky. "Why would I want to do that?"

"To stop us from leaving. Reyes Feliz would do it."

"I'm not Feliz."

"True, *senor*. But you work for Don Otero, or you did until last night. Now you work for his daughter, yes? Maybe you would shoot us for her."

"She doesn't tell me when to pull the trigger," Fargo said. "Quit beating around the bush. Why don't you come right out and say what is on your mind?"

Pedro exchanged a worried gaze with Felipe, then shrugged. "Very well. We have no choice. To put it simply, we want to head for Mexico and this is the only chance we may have to do it without the *bastardo* Feliz breathing down our necks." He paused. "We have wanted to leave for some time but two things stopped us. First, we felt loyal to our *patron*. Don Otero took good care of his people. But now he is dead and we are no longer obligated to stay."

"And the second thing?"

"Feliz. He has ridden herd on all the *vaqueros* since he was hired. Even Rojos is scared of him. And over a month ago Feliz vowed he would track down and kill anyone who deserted the Oteros."

Fargo recalled suspecting as much. "What about Gitana? Don't you want to stay and help her out?"

"With all due respect, *senor,* she is not as widely loved as her father. She is a temperamental girl in a woman's body. Not only that, everyone knows she has been sharing her bed with Feliz, and no self-respecting lady would do such a thing."

"Do you have proof of this?"

"No, *senor*. But the house servants know. They have seen Feliz sneaking from her bedroom early in the morning. Ask any of them and they will confirm it."

"How many of the *vaqueros* feel the way you do about leaving?"

"Many, but they are too afraid to say so for fear of Feliz,"

111

Pedro said. He leaned forward. "What do you say? Will you permit Felipe and me to ride off?"

"First tell me something," Fargo said. He wanted to learn exactly how much the *vaqueros* knew about the slave running operation.

"If I can."

"Why are the Apaches so determined to drive the Oteros from the valley?"

Pedro shifted uncomfortably. "Who can understand Apaches, eh?"

"If you want to head for Mexico, you'd better tell me the truth," Fargo warned.

The *vaquero's* shoulders slumped. He nervously twined his fingers together and gazed at the flowing water. "If Feliz should hear that I told you, he'll kill me."

"Feliz isn't going to hear a word."

"Very well," Pedro said, looking up. "You have the air of a man who can be trusted, so I will take the risk. I have heard stories that the Oteros have been selling Apaches as slaves to rich mine and land owners in Mexico. This has been going on for many, many years."

"All you've heard is stories? You've never actually seen it being done?"

"No, *senor.* We've worked for the Oteros about three and a half years now, but we've never been asked to take part in the night rides."

"The what?"

"Every now and then Rojos and fifteen or twenty of the older hands will ride off in the middle of the night and not return for many days. They never say where they have been, and anyone who asks is told to mind their own business," Pedro related. "Felipe and I had been here about two months when the first night ride took place. Naturally I was curious and I quietly asked around. No one would tell me a thing until I'd been here a year. Then one of the older *vaqueros*, Manuel, took a liking to me and confided in me that they were conducting raids on Apache villages and stealing men and women who could be sent to Mexico."

"Villages? They've been taking Apaches from more than one village?"

"*Si*. As far as I know. Three or four, at least."

"Apaches move around a lot. How does Rojos find these villages?"

"I don't know how they did it long ago, but until recently there was a *vaquero* by the name of Gallegos who worked here for many years, and some say he was one of the best trackers alive."

"What happened to him?"

"He was killed on the last raid some months back."

The revelation explained a lot. Fargo figured that the Otero family had used the services of Gallegos, and probably other trackers before him, to locate Apache villages ripe for raiding. Only senior *vaqueros*, those who had been with the Oteros for years and were the least likely to report the slave running to the authorities, were permitted to go on the raids. The Oteros probably paid them hefty bonuses as well.

Gallegos's death explained why the Oteros had desperately wanted to hire a new tracker. It explained the reason the Chiricahuas had not been attacked since moving to the top of the plateau. But it didn't explain why the Oteros wanted the Chiricahuas wiped out.

"It bothered me, *senor*," Pedro went on. "I felt guilty working for a man who did such a thing, but he paid so well that I overlooked it. Then the Chiricahuas began raiding us more and more, even going so far as to kill men riding herd at night, and I knew I could not stay any longer. I'm not a coward, *senor*. I just see no reason to let myself be killed over a matter that does not directly concern me. Do you understand?"

Fargo nodded. It had been all right for Pedro, Felipe, and other *vaqueros* to turn their backs on the slave operation so long as they were receiving high wages and there was no danger. But now that the Chiricahuas were carrying the fight to the Oteros, Pedro and company wanted out.

"Will you let us go?"

"I won't stop you."

Pedro grinned and spoke to Felipe in Spanish. They promptly stood and mounted their horses. Pedro looked down at the big man on the bank.

"We thank you, *senor*. In return I would give you a word of advice. You would be wise to ride out of the valley yourself.

It has been whispered around the bunkhouse that Feliz intends to kill you. He thinks you have eyes for Gitana Otero. The only reason you are still alive, I think, is because you are the best tracker they have at the moment. But if another should come along . . ." Pedro said, and left the thought unfinished.

"I appreciate the warning," Fargo said. "Are you sure you can find your way across the border with no problem?"

"Yes. There is a well-used trail south of the valley. We will be fine."

"Watch out for Apaches."

"Always." Pedro grinned, touched the brim of his *sombrero*, and rode off with Felipe at his side. They stuck to the stream until they rounded a low hill and disappeared.

Fargo watched them go, idly chewing on jerky. Bit by bit the answers he needed were coming out, but the information wasn't doing him much good. He still had no idea how he could be of any assistance to the Chiricahuas.

After eating he mounted up and made a leisurely circuit back to the valley. He passed within half a mile of the spot where he'd tangled with the three ambushers and spotted buzzards circling high above the corpses. Hopefully the carrion eaters would do their job before anyone from the *hacienda* found the remains.

He saw Indian sign here and there. Once he crossed the trail made by the band that had struck the house and the *vaqueros* who had pursued them. There were scores of hoof prints everywhere, the shod hooves of the hands' horses easily distinguished from the unshod Indian animals. The tracks led toward a ravine far to the west, undoubtedly the same one where the ambush had been sprung.

When at last he descended into the valley the afternoon sun was arcing down toward the horizon and the shadows had started to lengthen. Another day would soon be done and he was no closer to a solution than the day before.

He took his sweet time until he came within a hundred yards of the house. Then he spied six horses tethered near the front steps and goaded the Ovaro forward. Ordinarily he would assume they belonged to *vaqueros*, but these animals sported Texas rigs, not the Mexican saddles favored by the hands from south of the Rio Grande.

114

Fargo rode up to the six horses and went to swing down. Suddenly he heard gruff laughter and the front door opened. Out came six men, all hardcases. At the sight of him the leader, a bear of a man wearing a Colt high on his right hip, paused on the top steps and bellowed for all to hear: "Why, look at this, boys. Unless I'm mistaken, there sits the famous Trailsman. Rojos told us he's working here and it's said he rides a big pinto stallion." The man snorted in contempt. "They say this Trailsman is one of the toughest *hombres* around. Do you reckon we should kiss his boots or show him what real men are like?"

16

Rowdy laughter greeted the remark.

Fargo didn't need a formal introduction to know he was staring at the scourge of the Southwest, none other than Jesse Walker himself. The man had arrived well ahead of schedule.

Over six feet in height, his shoulders and thick neck muscles bulging even when he was standing still, Walker wore Levi's and a grimy white hat. He had a full beard and mustache, neither of which had been trimmed in a coon's age. An old, jagged scar slanted across his left cheek, resembling a miniature lightning bolt.

The five other hardcases were made from the same mold. All had rugged features. All wore dusty clothes. And all packed prominent hardware.

Fargo dismounted and ground-hitched the pinto. He faced the chuckling crowd at the top of the stairs and smiled. "As I live and breathe," he said sarcastically. "It must be Jesse Walker. I should have known you were here, though. I've been smelling a strange odor for the last mile or so."

All laughter ceased. Walker glowered and advanced to the bottom of the steps, his partners flanking him. "No man talks to me like that," he snapped. "Not if he likes breathing."

Fargo balled his fists. He didn't know why Walker had seen fit to insult him, but he felt an intuitive, intense dislike for the self-appointed rustling regulator. Something about Walker rubbed him the wrong way and he refused to let the prodding cutthroat ride herd over him. "I'll bet you're a terror at scaring ladies."

The next instant Walker waded into the Trailsman with his arms flying.

Retreating a step, Fargo blocked several powerful blows and delivered a punch to the hardcase's jaw that rocked Walker on his heels. He closed in, planting his left fist in Walker's gut and following up with a right to the mouth that knocked Walker down.

One of the other men started to close in, his right hand dropping to a knife on his hip.

"No!" Walker bellowed, rising on his elbows. He touched his right hand to his bleeding lips, then stared at the blood on his fingers. "This high and mighty son of a bitch is mine." Grunting, he pushed to his feet and held his fists at waist height. "I've heard a lot about you, Fargo. They say you're the best. Well, I've got news for you. *I'm* better." So saying, he tore into the Trailsman again.

Fargo deftly countered every swing and gave better than he got. They each stood their ground, raining blows, absorbing punishment that would have downed most men. Engrossed in the fight, he didn't realize others had joined them until a shrill feminine voice yelled and Gitana Otero, heedless of her own safety, rushed up to Walker, grabbed his shirt, and roughly pulled him to one side. Then she boldly stepped between them. "That's enough!" she declared. "What is the meaning of this? Why are you trying to kill each other?"

Fargo merely glared at his foe. If there was such a thing as love at first sight, then this qualified as hate at first glance. He could see unbridled hatred lurking in Walker's eyes and felt his anger rise.

Jesse Walker wiped his sleeve across his mouth and grinned. "Shucks, ma'am. We're just having a little manly fun, is all."

"Fun?" Gitana repeated, looking from one to the other. "You call beating each other to death fun?" She focused on Skye. "Do you have a grudge against Mr. Walker?"

"We've never met," Fargo said.

Gitana turned to Walker. "I don't understand. If this is the first time the two of you have laid eyes on each other, why were you fighting?"

"Do you know anything about roosters, ma'am?" Walker rejoined.

Puzzled by the question, Gitana nodded. "A little. Why?"

"Well, if you stick a pair of roosters together, odds are they'll tear into each other to prove who's the head of the roost, so to speak. The same holds true with some men. All it takes is one look and the feathers start to fly."

117

Gitana placed her hands on her hips. "I won't have it, do you hear? I've hired both of you to do a job, and until the job is finished you will keep your personal feelings to yourself. I want the two of you to work together, not kill each other. Is this understood, Mr. Walker?"

"Sure," Walker said, brushing at his shirt. "I have no objection to finishing this after our work here is done." He motioned for his men to follow and walked toward their horses. "We'll stow our gear in the bunkhouse and be ready to start when you give the word."

"Fine. Thank you," Gitana said.

Fargo watched them go. Sooner or later there would be a reckoning with Jesse Walker, a reckoning Walker clearly wanted. Why else had the hardcase brazenly insulted him? Anyone who lived on the frontier long enough knew that a man had to keep a tight rein on his mouth. The most innocent of comments, under the wrong circumstances, often led to bloodshed. And outright insults were guaranteed to incite trouble. Some men, like Walker, were known to provoke such incidents for the sheer hell of it. If this was the case now, then Walker would learn the hard way that he'd bitten off more than he could chew.

"I'm surprised at you, Skye," Gitana said. "I didn't think you were the type to indulge in senseless brawls."

He faced her and for the first time spied Rojos and Feliz standing on the lower steps. "And I didn't figure you were the type to take on killers like Walker. You must know his reputation. He causes more problems than he's worth. Rojos shouldn't have hired him."

"*Si*," Gitana said defensively. "I know of Mr. Walker's reputation. Why did you think I told Rojos to see if he could locate Walker and make him an offer?"

Fargo's lips compressed. The more he learned about her, the less he liked.

"I need a man of Walker's talents, just like I need a man of your talents," Gitana went on. "With you to find the Chiricahua village and Walker to oversee the raid, the Apaches don't stand a prayer. I will be rid of them once and for all."

"Speaking of which," Rojos interjected, coming down to stand beside her, "did you have any luck today?"

"No, I didn't come across the village," Fargo said, and then recalled he must cover for the two *vaqueros*. "And those two men you sent with me disappeared."

"What?" Rojos said, alarmed.

"Yep. The last time I saw them was by a little stream where they were resting and eating jerky. I saw Apache tracks all over the place."

"You became separated?" Rojos asked in surprise.

"It was their idea," Fargo said. "They wanted to cover more ground." He almost grinned at his deception. Every word he'd said was true, only the sequence of events was all out of order.

"This is bad news," Rojos stated. "While you were gone three riderless horses showed up. They belong to three of our men who have been missing since sometime the day before yesterday. I fear the Apaches got them, also."

"How I hate them!" Gitana said. "From now on the *vaqueros* are to stay in the valley. Tomorrow Skye will ride into the mountains with Walker and his men."

"I won't go anywhere with Walker," Fargo said.

"Be reasonable. You may not like him, but Walker can hold his own against Apaches. You will be safer with him along."

"No," Fargo said, "and that's final. Once I let you know where the village is situated, Walker can ride out and destroy it if the Chiricahuas will let him. But I won't work with the man." He stepped to the Ovaro and retrieved the Sharps. "If you don't like it, I'll ride out now."

"Don't be hasty," Gitana said. "I certainly wouldn't try to force you to do something you don't want to do. If you would rather ride alone, then go ahead and get scalped for all I care."

The big man brushed past her on his way up the steps. "Rojos, would you see that my horse is taken care of?"

"Of course, *senor*."

Annoyed at the turn of events, Fargo went inside and directly up to his room. He'd bought himself a little time to come up with a brainstorm by refusing to go with Walker, but if he didn't locate the village soon Rojos and Gitana would become increasingly suspicious. Depositing the rifle on the bed, he went into the bathroom and washed his face using the water in the basin. Slightly refreshed, he came out and abruptly halted.

Standing with her back to the closed door was Dolorita. She

held a finger to her lips and came over. "I only have a minute. Tonight I will come to you and tell you everything you want to know."

"I'll leave the door cracked," Fargo said.

She nodded and raced out.

Maybe the day wouldn't be a total waste, Fargo reflected. He waited a bit to give her time to get wherever she was going, then walked downstairs to see about getting a bite to eat.

Gitana and Rojos were standing in the hall near the sitting room, conversing in whispers. They stopped when he approached and the foreman excused himself and departed.

"Skye!" Gitana greeted him as if they'd never had an argument. "Would you do me the honor of joining me for supper?"

"I'd be glad to."

They went into the dining room and two servants began bringing out the food. Gitana chattered away, making small talk about the difficulties of managing a huge ranch. She wondered how she would get by without her father.

As Fargo listened, he thought about the news Pedro had imparted concerning Gitana and Feliz. All this time he'd assumed the attraction was largely one-sided; Feliz adored her but she hardly gave him the time of day. But if Pedro's information was true—and he had no reason to doubt it—it made him suspect she might have had an ulterior motive when she came into his room the other night. As he well knew, some women used sex as a weapon, as a means of getting men to do whatever they wanted, as a way of wrapping a man around their finger. Although Gitana didn't appear to be the type, what if she was? Maybe she had made love to him as a means of keeping him in line. Maybe she figured she'd have him on a leash like she did Feliz.

The meal was uneventful until near the very end. Then Gitana glanced up at him and smiled coyly. "I hope you won't mind my mentioning this, but some of those who work for me are puzzled by your failure to locate the Apache village."

"Are they?" Fargo responded, lifting a glass of water to his lips.

"Yes, and with good reason. We had a tracker here once named Gallegos. He was the best in all of Mexico. Why, he

would have found the village by now without any problem,"
Gitana said sweetly. "Naturally, since you are also supposed
to be one of the top trackers west of the Mississippi, my men
are disappointed it is taking so long."

"If your men think they can do any better, they're welcome
to try," Fargo said, smacking the glass down.

"I didn't mean to offend you," Gitana said hastily. "I simply
wanted to let you know."

Fargo knew better. He'd been right about her growing
suspicious. She was letting him know in her not-so-subtle way
that she entertained doubts and expected results. He was running
out of time in more ways than one.

"Would you care for dessert?" she asked.

"No, thanks. I want to get an early start again tomorrow,"
Fargo said. He excused himself and returned to his room to
await the maid. Not knowing when she would show, he left the
door open a crack and reclined on his back on the bed. He didn't
bother with the lamp; when she opened the door, any light might
give her away. And he kept the Colt strapped around his waist.
The incident with the *vaquero* had taught him not to relax his
guard for a minute.

Someone had tacked a sheet over the broken window to keep
out the insects and it fluttered now and then in the breeze. From
outside came muted voices and once, in the distance, the howl
of a coyote.

Fargo felt more frustrated than he had in ages. If he didn't
figure out what to do soon, it would be too late. He lay for the
longest time pondering, discarding ideas that wouldn't work,
and made up his mind that his best bet lay in letting events take
their own course and adjusting accordingly.

An hour went by.

Two.

If the maid intended to come, she was taking her sweet time
about it. He rose and stepped to the sheet. Although he couldn't
see a thing, he knew the stars were out and heard low voices
arising in several directions. The conversations were subdued,
as if the speakers feared talking too loudly. The hands must
be in fear of another Chiricahua attack.

A soft rustling sound came from his rear.

Fargo spun, his hands falling to his Colt. Just entering was

Dolorita, dressed in a white blouse and a black skirt. She quietly closed the door and walked over.

"I am much sorry I am so late," she said. "I had to give Gitana an excuse to get away."

"What did you tell her?"

"That I was sick," Dolorita said, smiling, her white teeth a sharp contrast to the murky room. She inched a little nearer. "Shouldn't you have a light on?"

"And maybe advertise I have a visitor? No," Fargo said, crossng his arms across his chest. He gestured at the bed. "Would you care to sit down or would you rather stand?"

She gazed at the soft quilt and hesitated.

Imagining that she was embarrassed at being alone with him in the dark, Fargo chuckled. "It's okay. We can stand."

"No," Dolorita said. "We should be comfortable." She walked over and sat down.

"Just a second," Fargo said. "I don't want to be interrupted." As he had the night before, he wedged chairs under each door to prevent anyone from slipping inside. Then he went to the bed and sat a proper distance from her to avoid making her nervous. He found her very attractive, but she was there at his request to give him important information; he wouldn't feel right trying to take advantage of her. "Okay. What can you tell me?"

She moved several inches nearer and spoke almost in a whisper. "You wanted to know about the investigation, yes?"

"Yes."

"I do not know most of everything," Dolorita said in her inaccurate English, "but I do know Don Otero was quite upset some months back when he heard the Mexican government had started investigating reports of a slave-running operation."

Fargo leaned toward her to hear better. Their faces were now a mere six inches apart and he swore he could feel her warm breath on his cheeks. He had to force himself to concentrate on the matter at hand.

"One day I was down in the wine cellar, at the back, when Don Otero and Rojos came down. They did not see me," Dolorita went on. She moved even closer.

"And?" Fargo prompted, his voice oddly husky.

"I heard Don Otero tell Rojos that the Mexican government

had no proof to tie him to the slavery. But he was concerned the Mexican government would begin at this end," she said, choosing her words with care.

Somehow Fargo's face moved to within an inch of hers.

"Rojos said they would have nothing to fear if the proof at this end were to be taken care of," Dolorita concluded.

For a few seconds Fargo stared into her lovely eyes. Then he realized she was finished and quickly asked, "Those were his exact words?"

"Yes, *senor.*"

"Call me Skye," Fargo said, the implications sinking in. At last he had the final piece to the puzzle. The Oteros were going to wipe out the Chiricahuas to prevent any of the tribe from talking to government investigators, even though the chances of it happening were slim. Not that the U.S. government gave a hoot about the welfare of the Indians, but if the Mexican government made an official request, the U.S. would be obligated to follow through, particularly if the press got wind of the investigation. Public sentiment could be easily swayed in favor of the Chiricahaus if the truth became known.

He realized there were still a few things he didn't know. For instance, why were the Oteros going only after the Chiricahuas? What about the other tribes they'd been raiding over the years? Were the others too far away to pose much of a threat? Or did it possibly have something to do with Chihuahua? After all, very few Apaches spoke English. Since Chihuahua did, maybe the Oteros rated him as a special threat. They were afraid army investigators might somehow get to question him and their entire operation would be uncovered.

At least, that was the only conclusion that made any sense to him. It was well known that Apaches occasionally came into towns throughout the region to trade or buy whiskey. Maybe Otero had been concerned word of any investigation would get back to Chihuahua and the chief would voluntarily ride into the nearest fort to report on the Otero slave operation. It would never have occurred to Chihuahua to do so before because the Apaches were not in the habit of running to the whites to settle their problems; they took care of such situations themselves.

"Does this help you?" Dolorita asked, reaching out and covering his hand with hers.

"Yes," Fargo replied, feeling the tips of her fingers lightly stroke his skin.

"I was so scared when I walked in here yesterday and saw Carlos trying to stab you," Dolorita said.

"Why would you care one way or the other about me?"

Dolorita took a deep breath before answering. "Because you have always been nice to me." She paused and lowered her voice. "And because you are a very handsome man, *senor.*"

"I told you to call me Skye," Fargo reminded her. He could resist temptation no longer. His lips descended on hers and she uttered a little moan. Then her arms came up and curled around his neck. She pressed herself against him as if hungry for passion and ran her fingers through his hair, dislodging his hat as she did.

Fargo's passion was fully aroused. He eased his right hand between their bodies and cupped her breasts, massaging each thoroughly, feeling the heat she generated in the palm of his hand.

Dolorita groaned and entwined her tongue with his. Her hands were everywhere; she couldn't seem to get enough of him.

Slowly Fargo pressed her back onto the quilt. He tugged at her blouse, pulling it loose from her skirt, and slid his hand under the fabric. Her skin burned to his touch, and his fingers closed on her right nipple and squeezed. She twisted under him and lifted her hips.

"Aaaaaahhh," she whispered. "So nice. I knew you would be nice."

He lifted her blouse so his lips could replace his fingers. At the first contact of his tongue with her nipple she arched her spine.

"Oh! Oh!" she said softly.

Fargo dawdled at her swelling globes, savoring the taste of them, stroking her fires for the main event. She cooed and purred almost inaudibly, apparently leery of making too much noise and being overheard. His right hand strayed to her knees and crept higher under the skirt, stroking her glossy thighs. To his surprise she wore no underclothes. Her legs parted to grant him access to her moist tunnel and he inserted his middle finger to the hilt.

124

"Yessss!" Dolorita breathed in his ear. "Do me, please. I have wanted you since first I laid eyes on you."

He licked her neck and locked his lips on hers while sliding his finger in and out. She swayed under him, her hips thrusting to meet his strokes. Her sleek inner thighs quivered, her breath coming out in short puffs. His organ strained at his pants, and he reluctantly removed his finger to strip off everything from the waist down.

She grinned at him as he positioned himself between her legs. "Gitana would kill me," she said, and giggled.

What did Gitana have to do with anything? Fargo idly wondered, and promptly forgot about it as he lowered his mouth to her nether lips and inserted his tongue.

Dolorita squealed, then clamped her hand over her mouth to keep from crying out. She bucked against his lips to the rhythm of his tongue and pressed her nubile thighs flush with his ears.

The big man licked and flicked until she was squirming uncontrollably. Only then did he rise up, align his throbbing member with her pleasure sheath, and ram himself into her as far as he could go.

Her eyes became the size of saucers and she half-lifted her torso off the bed. Her mouth widened as if she would scream; instead she sank back and coupled with the fire of a woman who had long been denied sensual ecstasy.

Pacing himself, Fargo did his utmost to please her. He pounded away, feeling tension form at the base of his spine and slowly travel along his loins. An inferno flared at the junction of their union, threatening to engulf them both.

"Please," Dolorita begged. "Please."

He thrust harder, the explosion building, and when at last the moment arrived, she bent upward and sank her teeth into his left shoulder to stifle a scream of primal joy. They rocked together until their erotic energy dissipated. In unison they collapsed. He rolled onto his right side and gulped in air, feeling marvelously invigorated.

She pecked him on the forehead, snuggled close, and closed her eyes.

About to do the same, Fargo became instantly aware when he heard a soft click from the direction of the corridor door.

He twisted and looked, uncertain whether someone had been trying to get in or not. As near as he could tell in the dim light, the chair was still braced in place and the door still closed. He waited a minute to be sure, then laid down and luxuriated in the afterglow of their union. For the moment he forgot all about his worries, all about the storm looming on his personal horizon.

There would be time enough for bloodshed tomorrow.

17

The next day got off to a good start.

Fargo awakened to the crowing of a rooster and found Dolorita gone. They had made love once more in the middle of the night and she had clung to him as if starved for affection. He hadn't known what to make of it and didn't embarrass her by prying.

Now he stood and went into the bathroom. In five minutes he was fully dressed, the Colt riding snug on his hip, the Sharps in his right hand, and making his way downstairs. Few of the servants were up. Thankfully, he saw no sign of Gitana.

Once outside he paused on the portico and inhaled the crisp fresh air. The sun had not yet risen and only a few farm hands and *vaqueros* were abroad. Neither Jesse Walker or his henchmen appeared to be up yet.

So far, so good, Fargo mused, and hurried to the stable to collect the Ovaro. He wasn't in the least bit hungry. Perhaps his lack of appetite had something to do with the fact he finally had a plan of action, a means of putting an end to the slavery once and for all, and he was eager to put the scheme into effect.

It had hit him after the second lovemaking of the night, as he lay quietly on his side and listened to Dolorita's soft breathing. Since the Oteros had seen fit to spring a trap on the Chiricahuas, why not return the favor? He couldn't hope to beat Walker, Feliz, and the *vaqueros* involved in the operation single-handedly. But he could turn the tables if he tricked Walker and the rest into riding into an Apache ambush.

As he put his saddle on the stallion, he mentally reviewed his brainstorm. He'd been able to get close to the Apache village once and figured he could do so again without entailing too great a risk. If he kept his eyes peeled, he was bound to see Nana or Nalin leaving the village for one reason or another. It should be a simple matter for him to catch up with them and explain his plan. Then they could relay the strategy to Chihuahua. If the chief liked it, the Oteros' slave running days were over.

And if not? Fargo frowned as he swung into the saddle. If not, he'd simply ride on out of the valley. He would have done the best he could under the circumstances. No man could do more.

He rode out, making for the distant mountains, checking behind him a few times to ensure no one was tailing him. He wouldn't put it past Walker to try and follow him all the way to the plateau. But other than a *vaquero* or two heading for the grazing land, no one showed.

The sun was peeking above the horizon by the time he came to the foothills. He rode hard, pushing the pinto, wanting to reach the village by midday. His main concern was running into bands of Apaches along the way. Except for Nalin, her brother, and the chief, the Chiricahuas would kill him on sight.

He thought about the scores, if not hundreds, of Apaches the Oteros had sold into slavery down through the years and wondered how anyone could stoop so low as to sell another human being for money. In the South it was common practice, he knew, for wealthy plantation owners to own black slaves brought from Africa and other countries. But just because some folks tolerated the practice didn't mean he had to.

Maybe his feelings had something to do with the life he lived. He deliberately shied away from civilization, preferring the solitude and freedom of the wilderness, of the uncharted regions of the West, to towns and cities where there were more laws governing behavior than there were people to misbehave. He liked the free life, where a man was his own master and could do as he pleased without someone breathing down his neck. Long ago he'd made up his mind that no one was going to tell him how to live, and he resented the notion that there were those who felt they had the God-given right to do just that.

The time passed quickly. Since Fargo knew the location of the village he could take the shortest possible route to the plateau. He approached it from the east this time and discovered a gradual, tree-covered slope led to the summit. His seasoned eyes detected a trail winding from the bottom to the top, evidently the route most frequently used by the Chiricahuas.

To avoid being seen, Fargo stuck to the trees, riding through the woods on the south side of the trail until he attained the summit where he stopped at the treeline to survey the terrain ahead. A quarter of a mile off was the village. He could see the wickiups, various Apaches moving around, and smoke curling from cooking fires. Dogs were playfully dashing to and fro.

Fargo decided to watch the village from there. He dismounted, led the stallion back into the forest so it couldn't be spotted from the trail, then tied the reins to a tree limb. Next he took the Sharps and walked to a point where the village was fully visible. Crouching behind a pine, he waited.

A party of four warriors rode to the south.

He studied the group, certain Nana wasn't among them. From his position he enjoyed a good view of both Chihuahua's and Nana's wickiup. Once he saw a woman go into the chief's and not reappear. But there was no activity at all near Nana's lodge.

Almost an hour went by.

Fargo tried to keep his impatience in check. He hopefully tracked the movements of every Indian he saw and realized there were few warriors present. The rest, he figured, must be out hunting.

Then he heard the horses.

A large body of mounts were ascending the east slope at a gallop, some neighing and snorting.

Lowering himself to the ground, Fargo turned toward the trail. He expected to see a band of Chiricahuas until he heard the creak of saddle leather and a few sentences spoken in Spanish. Stark astonishment shot through him when Jesse Walker and his men, Feliz, Rojos, and over a dozen well armed *vaqueros* appeared.

No! It couldn't be!

Fargo almost rose and began firing out of desperation. He observed them rein up just shy of the rim. Had they tracked him? He'd been extremely careful about leaving prints, and despite stopping every so often to check his back trail he'd not detected any hint of pursuit. How could they have done it?

Jesse Walker rose in the stirrups to scan the plateau, then reached into his saddlebags and pulled out a collapsible telescope. He extended it and focused on the village.

Now Fargo understood. A chill rippled down his back. He'd been a fool! Walker had used an old trick employed by the mountain men decades ago to keep tabs on Indians and buffalo movements. Toting telescopes had been quite common back then. Even Lewis and Clark had used them on their famous expedition. Telescopes enabled anyone to see for miles, and it must have been easy for Walker to trail Fargo while remaining so far back that Fargo couldn't hope to spot them.

Anger gripped him and he raised the Sharps to his shoulder. The moment they started forward he would open fire. The shots would give the Chiricahuas warning of the attack and might throw the *vaqueros* into confusion.

Walker lowered the telescope and replaced it in his saddle-bags. Drawing his revolver, he exchanged hushed words with Rojos and Feliz. Rojos, in turn, turned to the *vaqueros* and issued instructions.

Intent on sighting on Jesse Walker, Fargo didn't realize the *vaqueros* were fanning out on either side of the trail until the thud of hooves on the ground alerted him to a man heading directly at him. He looked up when the *vaquero* was only twenty feet away and their eyes met simultaneously.

The shocked *vaquero* held a revolver in his right hand. He opened his mouth to shout and extended his gun.

Fargo shot him. The heavy slug lifted the man clean out of his saddle to smash against a tree trunk. Shouts broke out and other *vaqueros* rode toward their companion. He quickly back-pedaled a good eight feet and stopped behind a different tree to load another round. Peeking out, he saw three *vaqueros* ringing the body and gazing nervously into the woods.

Beyond them Jesse Walker was leading most of the Otero hands in an abrupt change toward the village. Evidently the shot had convinced Walker there wasn't time to spread his men out in a flanking maneuver.

Damn it all, Fargo fumed. Nothing seemed to go his way. He stayed low and headed for the Ovaro, but he only went a few yards when a gun cracked and a bullet struck a limb above his head. Throwing himself to the right, he rolled until he came up against a boulder, hearing more shots that missed. In a swift motion he scrambled behind the boulder and rose to his knees.

The three *vaqueros*, their guns smoking, were coming after him.

He had no desire to kill the trio, but he couldn't get away with them after him. Snapping the rifle up, he aimed at the lead rider and squeezed the trigger. Again the Sharps blasted and a man went down.

The remaining pair saw smoke billow from the rifle barrel and immediately returned fire, recklessly blazing away at the boulder.

Fargo had to duck down as bullets zinged off in all directions. He flattened and crawled into a thicket, then angled to the east. A hasty glance showed him the *vaqueros* had dismounted and were creeping forward on foot.

Jesse Walker and the others were a hundred yards away and galloping in a ragged line toward the Apaches. The village was in turmoil with the warriors, women, and children frantically rushing about, many trying to catch horses, a few fleeing into the forest or heading around the lake. Some braves were rushing out to meet the attackers, most on foot.

The big man scowled and pressed onward. He rued the day he'd ever met Rojos and agreed to work for the Oteros.

One of the *vaqueros* shouted and a gun boomed.

Fargo heard the bullet whiz past. He rolled onto his back, the rifle clutched in his left hand, and saw a man in a black sombrero foolishly running at him while trying to hold a revolver steady. In a flash he drew the .44 and banged off two shots the very second the man fired. His shots caught the *vaquero* high in the chest; the *vaquero's* bullet hit the dirt inches from his right ear.

The last man was circling to the left, trying to get a clear shot.

Skye pointed his Colt at a spot between two trees the *vaquero* was approaching, cocked the hammer, and when the man stepped into his sights he squeezed the trigger. His shot took the man in the side of the head, spinning the *vaquero* completely around before the man toppled over.

He shoved upright and ran to the Ovaro. Swiftly mounting, he rode to the trail and stared at the village. The Otero men were already there, sweeping in among the wickiups with their guns thundering in a lethal chorus of shattering sound. It appeared that most of the Chiricahuas had wisely fled into the surrounding trees but a few warriors were gamely putting up a fight, the majority using bows, two or three firing rifles. They were slaughtered where they stood. So were several women and children who didn't flee fast enough. Camp dogs were likewise shot to pieces.

The Trailsman observed the massacre for all of five seconds. He worked the trigger guard on the Sharps, which exposed the chamber, and fed in a new cartridge. Then, his face set in grim lines, he goaded the stallion forward. He saw some of the Chiricahuas being herded into the center of the village by smirking *vaqueros* and curled his finger around the trigger. Not that he stood a prayer against so many men; he simply had to do something.

At full gallop the big stallion reached the village in less than half a minute, but by the time Fargo got there the one-sided battle had concluded and there were five frightened but stoic Apaches ringed by gun barrels in the center of the village and over a dozen bodies dotting the ground, not counting the dogs that had been shot.

A few *vaqueros* glanced at Fargo as he rode up but made no move to shoot him. He realized none of the others had seen him in the trees. For all they knew he was just arriving on the scene.

"Well, lookee here," bellowed a gruff voice off to the left.

Fargo reined up. Coming around the corner of a wickiup were Jesse Walker, two of his men, Reyes Feliz, and Jose Rojos. Surprisingly, Feliz actually smiled.

"So you finally found the village," Walker said, coming to a stop. "But you're a little late to take part in the fun. Of course, you could join the rest of the *vaqueros* in chasing down those Apache vermin."

Rojos moved his mount a little closer. "Before you say a word, *Senor* Fargo, allow me to explain. We followed you this morning when you left the *hacienda*. Frankly, none of us expected you to find the village, but you did. We saw you ride onto this plateau and came up to investigate. Once we spied the Apaches we immediately decided to attack. We figured you were making a circuit of the village to determine their strength, and we couldn't afford to delay by sending someone to find you." He paused to smugly survey the carnage. "Not a bad day's work, no?"

Before the big man could answer, Reyes Feliz moved his horse beside the Ovaro, still smiling at Fargo as if at his best friend, and motioned at one of the bodies. "Too bad you didn't come sooner. But then you must be tired from all that riding and staying up so late." He slyly winked.

Suddenly Fargo understood the *pistolero's* friendliness. He *had* heard someone at the bedroom door last night; Feliz, probably checking to see if Gitana had been in the room. Somehow Feliz had guessed Dolorita was there, and now the man in black believed that Fargo was interested in the maid, not Gitana.

Walker pointed at the five prisoners, three women and two children. "Since you missed out, why don't you go first and show us what that big rifle of yours can do to squaws?"

"Let them go."

"What?" Walker said, looking at Rojos and Feliz. "Why should we do that?"

"Women and children are no threat to the Otero ranch. Just let them leave in peace."

"Can't do that," Walker said, his right hand straying to his hip within inches of the revolver. "Indian brats grow up to become murderous bucks, and squaws breed like rabbits. The best thing to do is kill every last one of them, exterminate them like you would rats."

Fargo glanced at the captives, his jaw muscles hardening. Then he squared his shoulders and let his reins rest on the pommel so his hands would be free. "No one is touching a hair on their heads."

"I do not understand, *senor,"* Rojos said. "You were hired to help us fight the Apaches."

"I was hired to help you find their village, not to butcher innocent women and children," Fargo corrected him.

"I understand perfectly," Jesse Walker stated.

"You do?" Rojos asked.

"Yep. Do you remember that shot we heard when we were starting to fan out back there by the rim?" Walker said.

"*Si,*" Rojos answered, perplexed.

"Only one kind of gun makes a sound like that," Walker said. "A Sharps." He looked at his two men and made a bobbing movement with his chin. They promptly moved off a few feet to the side. Leaning forward, Walker locked his eyes on the Trailsman's. "I never pegged you for an Indian lover, but I guess it takes all kinds. When I heard that you were working for the Oteros, I figured you'd have the village located by the time we reached the valley. When I heard you hadn't, it made me a mite suspicious. A man of your talents and you can't find a stinking nest of Indians? Then, when we trailed you today, it amazed me how you were able to make a beeline for this plateau without once studying the ground for tracks."

"You think you have it all figured out," Fargo said.

"I know you've been here before, yet you never told the Oteros. Why, I asked myself? The only reason I could think of is that you didn't want the Apaches to be found. You're on their side."

Walker's two men visibly tensed. Rojos still appeared puzzled. Feliz was gazing at Walker, digesting his words.

"Wait until I inform Miss Otero," Walker said. "I doubt she'll be inclined to pay you a cent."

"Tell her whatever you want," Fargo said. "But you're not harming these Apaches."

"Well," Walker said slowly, "I reckon we have something to say about that, don't you?" He nodded at his two men.

Both clawed for their hardware.

Fargo swept the Sharps up and fired, his slug tearing through the nearest rider's abdomen and blowing out the base of the man's spine. Even as he fired, Fargo kneed the Ovaro into motion. His right hand swept to the Colt and cleared leather as the second hardcase was doing the same. His shot cracked first, flinging the man off the back of his mount, and he shifted to train the .44 on Walker.

Suddenly a tremendous blow struck him on the back of the head and the last thing he remembered was pitching headfirst to the ground.

18

Fargo came awake slowly, painfully, his head throbbing, his arms and shoulders in agony. He could understand the reason his head hurt, but not his limbs. Slowly opening his eyes, he took a moment to orient himself in the dim light and promptly discovered the reason for his discomfort. His wrists were bound so tightly the rope was cutting into his flesh, and someone had gone to all the trouble to loop another rope from his wrists to a large wooden beam overhead, then over the beam to a hook on the wall to his left. His boots dangled several feet above a dirt floor. His Colt was gone. Lying a few feet to the right was his hat.

The pungent odor of horse manure hit his nostrils and he glanced around to discover stalls on both sides. A few Mexican saddles were draped over one, leading him to deduce he was hanging in a corner of the Otero stable. Twisting, he could see the entrance off to his right. Beyond stood the house.

One of the horses whinnied.

A group of figures materialized in the doorway and came toward him.

He recognized Gitana, Feliz, Rojos, and Walker. By shaking his right boot he could tell that his throwing knife had also been taken. Whoever searched him had done a thorough job.

"He doesn't look so high and mighty now, does he?" Jesse Walker gloated as they drew to a stop. "I say we whittle him down to size right now."

Gitana had her hands on her hips and was studying the Trailsman intently. "I will decide Skye Fargo's fate, not you, *gringo*," she snapped.

Walker glared at her. "There's no need to be insulting, ma'am. I work for you, so whatever you decide is just fine."

"Be sure that you remember it at all times," Gitana said, and stepped closer to Fargo. "I can't say that I am surprised at how things have turned out. I began to suspect you were not doing as I wanted a day or so ago.''

''Took you that long, did it?'' Fargo responded.

Without warning Feliz walked up and slugged the big man in the pit of the stomach, causing Fargo to wheeze and sputter. ''You will address *Senorita* Otero with respect or answer to me,'' he growled.

Fargo grit his teeth and whipped his legs out, catching Feliz in the chest and knocking him backward.

In a flash Feliz went for his gun, but before he could draw Gitana stepped between them.

''That will be enough!'' she declared. ''If you can't control your temper, leave.''

The man in black glowered, then eased his hand off his revolver. ''Very well. But when the time comes, I want to be the one to put a bullet between his eyes.''

''Tired of letting others do your dirty work for you?'' Fargo baited him.

Gitana looked up. ''What do you mean?''

''Who do you think put Carlos up to trying to kill me? Who did you think had three of your *vaqueros* try to bushwhack me in the foothills? And who do you think tried to kill me the other evening when we were on the back porch?''

She turned to the man in black, incensed, her eyes angry slits. ''Is that true, Reyes?''

Feliz opened his mouth to reply, as if about to dispute the allegation, then changed his mind. Instead, he simply nodded.

''How could you? You tried to kill him without my permission?''

''I am sorry, *senorita.* ''

A contemptuous laugh came from Jesse Walker. ''You had your nerve criticizing me, missy, when you can't even keep your own men in line.''

Reyes glanced at the regulator. ''This doesn't concern you, killer. Mind your own business.''

''And what if I don't?'' Walker retorted.

Gitana raised her arms and shouted out, ''Enough! We are all on the same side. I will not have us arguing among ourselves, not when our work hasn't been completed.''

"It will be soon," Walker promised. "We'll find where Chihuahua is holed up and finish the job nice and proper."

Fargo had been all but forgotten in their heated exchange. He kept hoping Walker and Feliz would tear into each other and give him one less problem to deal with if he escaped. "So it is Chihuahua you're after," he remarked. "You must be afraid he'll talk if the U.S. government starts an investigation into slavery operations involving Apaches."

"How do you know about that?" Gitana asked in surprise.

"I know all about it," Fargo said. "About the fact your family has been selling Apaches for generations, about the investigation down in Mexico, the whole thing."

"Then you're smarter than I gave you credit for being. But your knowledge will go with you to your grave."

"Should I shoot him?" Feliz inquired hopefully.

"No," Gitana said. "Not yet. Mr. Fargo is a man of some reputation, as we all are aware. If he was to turn up with a bullet hole, there might be questions asked or friends of his would come looking for his killer." She paused. "I have a better idea. We'll arrange his death so that the Apaches are blamed. Everyone in Tucson knows he was hired by Rojos; everyone knows about the Indian trouble we've been having. It would be only natural for the savages to kill him."

"I like the notion," Walker said. "You have a real sneaky mind, just like me."

"I'll take that as a compliment," Gitana said, and pointed at the entrance. "Now I want all of you to go and leave me alone for a few minutes with Fargo."

"But . . . " Feliz began.

"Just go," Gitana insisted. "And Rojos, make certain that those guards you posted only permit hands who are familiar with our operation into the stable. Have them use whatever excuse you like. After all the trouble you went to smuggling Mr. Fargo in here, I don't want anyone else to know."

"*Si*. No one will get in," the foreman vowed.

The three men departed, Feliz with obvious reluctance. He repeatedly glanced over his shoulder at Fargo.

Moving closer, Gitana placed a hand on the big man's leg. "I am sorry at the way things have worked out between us.

I like you, Skye. I truly do. You know how to satisfy a woman, to bring out the fire in her." She sighed. "Few men do."

"Don't pretend with me," Fargo said. "You'd do anything to keep your precious valley safe. Lie, cheat, go to bed with a man, anything."

Gitana never batted a lash. "True. I take after my father. He let nothing stand in his way, and he taught me the only way to survive is to do the same. He told me to eliminate threats before they become a danger."

"Why not let Chihuahua and the rest of the Chiricahuas go? I doubt he'll even hear of the investigation. Maybe he'll fade farther back into the mountains and leave you alone."

"Perhaps. Perhaps not. I can't take the risk of having everything I've worked so hard for destroyed."

"You have nothing to worry about. The government wouldn't prosecute a woman. Hell, you know as well as I do that they don't care about the Apaches. They don't care about any of the tribes as long as the Indians behave themselves."

Gitana lowered her arm. "It is too late to stop now. I have too much time and money invested in wiping out the Chiricahuas. The men are going back out tomorrow to try and track the ones who fled from the village."

"How will you track them without me?"

"A *vaquero* named Valdez arrived here this morning while you were gone. We sent for him a few months ago. He's not in your class but he can track competently. So you see, it's almost over," she said, bestowing a look of compassion on him as she sashayed off. "Your sacrifice has been for nothing."

Fargo watched her leave. Outside it was growing dark and lamps had been lit in the house. He craned his neck to study the ropes securing his wrists but couldn't see them clearly. Wrenching on the bindings proved fruitless; they merely dug deeper into his flesh. And the thickness of the rope looped over the beam convinced him that attempting to break it by swinging back and forth to exert more pressure would be equally futile.

He had to face it. He was in a first-class bind with no apparent way out. For over an hour he hung there, unable to do anything else, until he heard footsteps and glanced at the stable entrance.

Coming toward him were Reyes Feliz and Dolorita, the

former carrying a lantern. She carried a tray containing a plate, a glass of water, and a white cloth. Her face became lined with anxiety when she saw him.

"Still here, I see?" the man in black said, and deposited the lantern near the east wall. "Against my wishes Senorita Otero has seen fit to give you a final meal. Were it up to me I would shoot you and get it over with."

"I reckon you would," Fargo said.

Feliz leered. "You should be nicer to me. I was the one who thought to have your sweetheart deliver the food."

Dolorita looked at him. "So that is why you asked me to bring this tray."

"Of course. I know all about the two of you. I thought this *gringo* had an interest in Gitana so I watched his room last night and every so often listened at the door," Feliz said. "I saw you go in." He snickered and slapped his thigh. "I must admit I expected you to have better taste."

Her features flushing crimson, Dolorita snapped at the gunman in Spanish. Feliz replied in kind and a lengthy argument ensued.

Fargo wanted to get his hands on Feliz's neck. The son of a bitch didn't bring Dolorita to the stable out of kindness; Feliz had done it as a sort of perverse prank, to mock Fargo and humiliate the maid.

The argument ended when Feliz barked orders at Dolorita and nodded at the Trailsman. He then stepped into a nearby stall and emerged with a short wooden stool. "Use this and you can reach his mouth," he said.

Dolorita positioned the stool on the big man's left side and stepped up. She gazed fondly into his eyes and lifted the glass of water. "I am sorry."

"Does Gitana know you're here?"

"I don't think so. I was working in the kitchen when Feliz came in and got me."

The Trailsman glanced at the *pistolero,* the germ of an idea taking shape. He deliberately raised his voice and declared, "Be sure and tell Gitana when you go back to the house. Then watch the fireworks. Feliz isn't allowed to breathe without her saying so."

The insult had the desired effect on the quick-tempered Feliz. He stalked toward Fargo, his fists clenched. "Let's see how well you eat without teeth."

"My sentiments exactly," Fargo said, tensing his arms and stomach muscles, waiting for the exact moment. He'd already kicked Feliz once and the *pistolero* would be wary of another try.

"Don't," Dolorita said, stepping down. "Please."

"Out of my way," Feliz said gruffly, and gave her a shove that sent her onto her backside, the tray flying from her hands. He halted next to Fargo and drove his right fist into the Trailsman's abdomen. "Gitana stopped me earlier. Now I will beat you senseless."

Agony radiated through Skye's body. Grunting, he bent his head down, struggling to control the waves of torment. He saw Feliz draw the fist back for another blow. At that moment, when Feliz believed he was incapable of striking back, Fargo did so. He swept both knees up and in, smashing them into Feliz's jaw, crunching the gunman's teeth together and making Feliz stagger backward in shock and pain. For an instant Fargo swung his legs back as far as he could, then arced forward, bringing both feet up and into the *pistoler's* face, his boots crushing Feliz's nostrils, the impact sending the man in black flying into the corner where he collapsed in a crumpled heap.

Dolorita had her hand pressed to her mouth.

"Quickly," Fargo urged. "Cut me down."

"But I have nothing to cut with."

"*Find* something."

Nodding, she rose and swiftly went into each of the nearest stalls. He could hear her rummaging about and glanced at the far end of the stable, afraid the guards had heard. A *vaquero* was leaning against the doorway, standing directly under a lantern and staring toward the house, a rifle cradled in his arms.

Dolorita reappeared holding a small knife of the kind typically used to repair saddles. She ran up to him. "Will this do?"

Fargo nodded. "It will have to. Put out the lantern so the guards can't see you and climb up. Hurry."

She dutifully complied, plunging the rear of the stable into darkness. It took her a moment to find the stool and step on it. Then she leaned against Fargo and stretched to grip the rope above his wrists, her body flush with his. She went to work with a vengeance. "This knife is not so sharp."

"Do the best you can," Fargo advised.

Breathing heavily from her exertions, Dolorita sliced at the strands, parting a few. "It will take a while," she said.

"We don't have all night," Fargo mentioned, and stiffened when he heard someone call out in Spanish from the vicinity of the entrance. "What did he say?"

Dolorita had stopped cutting. "It's one of the guards," she breathed. "He wants to know why the lantern was turned off."

"Damn," Fargo snapped. "Keep going."

Again she applied the knife to the rope, her warm breath fanning his face, her body swaying with every slice. She grunted, feverishly cutting, cutting, cutting.

The guard shouted again.

"He wants to know why Feliz hasn't answered," Dolorita translated in a panic. "And he's coming this way."

19

"Keep cutting," Fargo said, trying to see past her and up the aisle. The *vaquero* with the rifle was walking briskly toward them. He gazed down at Feliz and distinguished the pale outline of the pearl grips on the gunman's Dragoon. If only he could get his hands on that gun!

Dolorita sawed at the rope as if her life depended on it. A second strand parted, then another, and the more she cut, the easier the slicing became. She had no way of knowing how far into the rope she'd gone, and she was startled when the remaining strands parted with a soft snap and the big man dropped to the ground.

The fall also took Fargo by surprise, although he had the presence of mind to bend at the knees as he landed and stayed upright. He was down, but rope still bound his wrists. The *vaquero* was halfway there. Instead of trying for the Dragoon, he slid to the side and pressed his back to a stall. Bunching both hands into a single fist, he waited.

The *vaquero* called out once more.

Afraid the man's shouts would draw too much attention, Fargo whispered to Dolorita. "Tell him the lantern went out and Feliz doesn't have a match."

Still perched on the stool, she gamely did as he wanted, doing her level best to keep her voice calm and natural.

The *vaquero* said something else and laughed. He was nearly there.

Fargo raised his arms as he might if he was going to swing a club, and when a shadowy figure stepped into view he took a pantherish bound and struck the guard squarely on the face. The *vaquero* staggered backward, releasing the rifle and wildly clutching at thin air in a vain attempt to keep his footing.

Pressing his advantage, Fargo reached the guard just as the man landed on his posterior. A flick of Fargo's boot flattened

142

the *vaquero* cold. He knelt and felt along the guard's waist until he found a hip gun. Pivoting, he went over to the maid, whose white blouse made her stand out in the gloom. "Get this rope off my wrists."

Dolorita stepped down and used her free hand to feel along his forearms until she established the exact position of the rope. Then she placed the edge of the knife to work, being careful not to press too hard for fear of slicing Fargo's wrists open.

The big man listened for other guards. There must be more than one because Gitana had said as much. He impatiently strained at the rope, trying to snap it.

"What will you do now?" Dolorita whispered.

"Find my horse and guns and cut out. And you should come with me."

"I can not."

"They might figure out that you helped me."

"Gitana would never hurt me."

"I wouldn't put anything past her," Fargo said, continuing to strain his arms outward in the hope of breaking free. He figured the Ovaro was somewhere in the stable, his guns either in the house or the bunkhouse. Retrieving them might be impossible. If so, he'd make do with the guard's rifle and revolver and the Dragoon. Because although he was lighting out, the fight wasn't over by a long shot. He'd hound the Otero spread mercilessly, if that's what it took to bring Gitana down. Going to the authorities would be a waste of time; the government wouldn't care about Apaches being sold into slavery. No, he had to handle this himself.

The knife abruptly severed the rope.

Fargo wedged the revolver under his belt and rubbed his wrists to restore the circulation. His fingers tingled. Crossing to Feliz, he lifted the Dragoon from the *pistolero's* holster and slid it into his own. Next he found the rifle, then his hat, and faced the entrance.

Oddly, there was still no sign of another guard. "Did you see another *vaquero* out there?"

"*Si.* When I came in one man was sitting with his back to the wall, on the left side. He was dozing, I think."

"Stay behind me," Fargo cautioned, and advanced down the left side of the aisle, keeping close to the stalls in case he had

143

to dive for cover. Most of the stalls were occupied. He found the pinto in the fifth one back from the doorway, bathed in the edge of the glow from the lantern that hung on a hook at the entrance. The pinto whinnied and nuzzled at his shoulder and he gave it a pat on the head.

Motioning for Dolorita to stop, Fargo moved forward until he could peek out at the guard. Sure enough, there sat a hefty *vaquero* whose chin rested on his chest. Overhead were stars. From the house came laughter and loud voices. A few farm hands were crossing the yard but they paid no attention to the stable.

He returned to Dolorita. "Go out there and ask the guard to come in."

"Be careful."

Fargo followed her, then slipped into the first stall beside a mare that tossed its head and stamped a hoof but made no other sounds. He left the stall door parted a crack and crouched, listening to Dolorita address the guard. The man grumbled and rose, his spurs jingling, then entered.

The big man saw the *vaquero* walk past his hiding place. Instantly he swung the stall door wide, stepped out, glanced at the yard to be sure there were no witnesses, and slammed the rifle stock into the back of the man's skull.

Without uttering a word the *vaquero* toppled, hitting the dirt with a muted thud.

Working rapidly, Fargo dragged the guard into the first stall and secured the latch. Dolorita stood at the entrance, nervously observing the proceedings. "Will you change your mind about coming with me?"

"No. I would only slow you down. And I am confident Gitana will not harm me, no matter how mad she becomes."

"I suppose you know best . . ."

They shared a brief, lingering look. Dolorita spun and hastened toward the porch.

Fargo didn't bother to watch her go. He spied his saddle, along with five others, draped over the wall of a stall across the aisle. Darting over, he gripped it and went to the Ovaro. Saddling up took a minute, and then he was mounted, the rifle in his left hand, and moving slowly toward the entrance.

Two *vaqueros* were walking from north to south. One of the men glanced at the stable and froze.

Knowing what would happen next, Fargo prodded the big stallion out into the open and jerked the reins to the left. The *vaqueros* began shouting at the top of their lungs, drew their pistols, and ran to intercept him. Pressing the rifle to his shoulder, he squeezed off a shot that whirled one man in his tracks and prompted the second to try and kiss the earth.

He clasped the reins and started to cluck the stallion into a trot but detected movement out of the corner of his eye, a hint of someone racing at him from out of the depths of the stables. Shifting, he saw Reyes Feliz at the very moment the *pistolero* reached the guard sprawled in the aisle.

Feliz squatted, his face a bloody mess, his nose a shattered ruin, and grabbed the revolver in the unconscious guard's holster. He looked at the Trailsman as he whipped the gun up.

Fargo had the rifle in his left hand on the pinto's off side. His right leaped to the Dragoon and the heavy revolver leaped clear. The gun kicked in his hand when he fired, the booming retort beating Feliz's own shot by a hair.

Reyes Feliz was flung rearward, his arms outstretched, a crimson hole in his chest in line with the heart. He landed on his back and lay still, his mouth slack like that of a dead fish, his blank eyes fixed on the roof beams.

The big man holstered the Dragoon and bore to the south. He could forget retrieving his own hardware. He'd be lucky to get away with his life.

Already people were spilling from the house and the bunkhouse, some strapping on weapons, most yelling in confusion. Jesse Walker and his men appeared on the portico. They spotted the Trailsman and blazed away.

Bullets smacked into a tree on Fargo's left as he skirted the trunk. He rode on, not bothering to return their fire, realizing they would all be after him soon, in frenzied pursuit, eager for revenge.

He hoped Dolorita was right about Gitana not hurting her. In his estimation the maid was taking too much for granted, but he couldn't very well try to cart Dolorita off into the mountains against her will with a pack of killers on his trail.

145

There were harsh shouts behind him and a tremendous commotion as men dashed to the stable. Gitana Otero's voice rose above the din, issuing commands.

A half-moon hung in the heavens, providing feeble illumination, enough for Fargo to recognize obstacles and avoid them. He soon came to the road and bore westward. Once he put enough distance behind him, he was confident he could easily elude his pursuers.

The pounding of hooves drummed in the night, much sooner than he'd anticipated, and he glanced over his shoulder to find seven or eight men racing to overtake him. He slid the rifle into his saddle holster and brought the Ovaro to a gallop, hunching over the saddle, blending his body to the horse. If he sat upright his silhouette would be a tempting target. As it was, one of the riders snapped off two shots that missed.

Fargo had no definite destination in mind. Simply reaching the foothills was his main concern. On the flat land he had little hope of escaping; in the rugged upper elevations were plenty of places where he could hole up until daylight. He looked back and saw another party of riders leaving the *hacienda*. Several of the men carried lamps.

A grim, extended chase across the range ensued. The Trailsman stayed barely ahead of the seven men. Farther back was the main body.

The Ovaro's superb endurance served Fargo in good stead. Never once did it falter, and by the time they reached the base of the foothills the stallion was hardly breathing heavy at all. He urged it up a gradual slope, winding among huge boulders on either side.

A rifle cracked, the bullet whining off a boulder within a foot of his head.

He came to the crest and immediately plunged down the far side, digging his heels into the stirrups to retain his balance. This side was steeper and the Ovaro slid the final two dozen feet to the bottom, raising a cloud of dust in its wake.

"Down here!" someone at the top bellowed.

Fargo turned to the left, staying in a narrow gap between the hill he'd just crossed and another one. Shots punctured the night above him and lead smacked into the ground all around the stallion. He reached a level tract and reined to the right.

"This way!" a man yelled to his rear. "This way!"

The big man pressed on into the wilderness. After traveling a quarter of a mile he checked over his shoulder and saw the group of seven persistent riders still on his trail. Not only that, the second group, those using the lamps, were likewise still in pursuit.

He needed to do something to discourage them. Another hill materialized ahead and he rode to the top, then stopped and quickly dismounted. Since he'd already fired the rifle, an old Halls' single-shot, he palmed the Dragoon and turned to watch the seven riders draw even closer. They were soon at the bottom of the hill and starting upward.

Fargo let them get a third of the way up before he pointed the barrel into the thick of the group and fired. A man shrieked and seemed to fall. The rest halted abruptly and employed their own weapons, shooting furiously. He fired again. This time a horse whinnied and collapsed. Unnerved, the remaining riders scattered for cover.

The Trailsman spun, slipping the Dragoon into his holster, and ran to the pinto. Forking the saddle, he made off at a gallop with a grin creasing his lips, certain he'd bought himself enough time to make good his getaway.

In due course he went over a series of increasingly higher hills. The air became crisp and cooler. There was no hint of pursuit, and in an hour's time he began seeking a spot where he could rest until morning. Eventually he found it, a cluster of enormous boulders on the south side of a jagged peak. He rode into the middle of the boulders and found a spot where he could stretch out.

Sliding down, Fargo took a seat and considered his prospects. The Otero bunch would likely give up the chase by morning, if not sooner, and return to the *hacienda*. There would still be Apaches abroad, though, and except for Chihuahua, Nana, and Nalin they were all his enemies. If he stayed in the mountains he risked losing his hair.

But he certainly couldn't hide out in the valley where the *vaqueros* were bound to find him. His best bet seemed to be to stay on the move, stick to the foothills, never use any spot as a camp twice, and grow eyes in the back of his head.

The events of the day had fatigued him greatly. He reclined

on his back, the hard ground as comfortable as any mattress ever made, and closed his eyes. It was too bad he hadn't eaten some of the food Dolorita had brought to the stable; he was starved.

A soft breeze from the northwest whispered among the boulders, lulling him to sleep.

Fargo dozed, but he repeatedly woke up during the next half-hour to rise on his elbows and listen. The silence reassured him. He'd given the riders the slip. He settled down one last time and gazed at the sparkling canopy of stars above him.

Far to the southwest a coyote yipped. Another, closer, answered the plaintive yowl.

The big man propped his hands under his head and sighed. The first order of business tomorrow would be to ride to the village and see if any of the Apaches had returned. He doubted it, but he wanted to find Chihuahua and that was the logical place to start.

Soon Fargo's eyelids fluttered and he sank into sleep.

The sun had risen an hour above the horizon when Fargo was awakened by a slight noise and sat up with a start. His right hand fell to the Dragoon and he listened intently.

From beyond the boulder, to the east, came a faint scraping sound.

He surged upright and drew the revolver, then moved cautiously between two boulders until he could see part of the area surrounding his hideaway. There, heading at a leisurely pace to the north, were three black-tailed deer. He was tempted to shoot one for his breakfast, but the shot might attract unwanted attention.

Returning to the Ovaro, he replaced the Dragoon, mounted, and rode to the north himself. The deer heard him, looked back, and promplty bolted toward a stand of timber.

The brisk morning air invigorated him. He rode until he reached a stream, where he let the pinto quench its thirst and did the same himself. Deciding to wait until midday to eat, he continued toward the plateau, soon spying it to the northwest.

As he crested a barren hill peaked by huge slabs of rock and a few stunted trees, he saw the trail of shod tracks left by

Walker's party the day before when they raided the village. He didn't pay much attention to them until he was halfway down the hill. Then he gazed at the tracks again and received a shock.

Some of those prints weren't a day old.

Some had been made in the past few hours.

But by who?

At that moment, from below him, several guns blasted.

20

The air swarmed with lead. Fargo's hat was snatched from his head. An intense stinging sensation flared in his left cheek and invisible fingers plucked at his right sleeve. He cut to the left and took shelter behind a rock slab as more guns cut loose.

Sliding down, Fargo moved to the edge of the slab. He waited for the firing to cease before venturing a look. Drifting puffs of gun smoke marked the area where the gunmen were concealed, a dense section of pines on the next slope. He saw no one. Since only guns had been used, he concluded the ambushers must be from the Otero ranch.

A clatter of hooves drew his attention off to the left. Four *vaqueros* burst from the trees and rode around the base of the hill on which Fargo stood. They vanished from view before he could bring a revolver to bear. Alarmed, Fargo quickly made his way to the summit, threading among the slabs. Dropping flat just below the crest, he peered over the rim in time to see the quartet concealing themselves in a stand of trees and heavy brush.

He was trapped. Scowling, he returned to the Ovaro and pondered his next move. The *vaqueros* must have all sides of the hill covered. If he tried to escape during broad daylight, he'd be riddled with holes before he got to the bottom. Making a rough guess, he calculated there were no more than ten men in the group. Why were they there? He'd expected all of the hands to be back on the ranch.

The sound of another horse riding off prompted him to gaze at the facing slope. A lone *vaquero* was galloping toward the plateau. There could only be one reason. The man was going for others.

So that was it. Someone, Walker or Rojos or Gitana herself, had stationed men at various points near the plateau in the hope that he would appear. He wanted to kick himself for playing right into their hands.

Two shots cracked below and slugs struck the rock slab within inches of Fargo's face. He jerked backward, drew the Dragoon, and went to shoot back, then hesitated. Since he was hemmed in, it would be wise to conserve his ammunition.

He squinted up at the sun, feeling its heat on his skin. Once darkness descended he would try to escape, but until then there were ten hours or so of daylight remaining in which the *vaqueros* might try to overwhelm him.

Fargo went to his saddlebags and checked his spare ammunition. Fortunately the Dragoon and the revolver he'd taken from the other guard, a 1847 Colt, were both .44 caliber and could take the same ammo as his own pistol. He verified that the early model was fully loaded, then reloaded the Dragoon.

At least he'd be able to put up a hell of a fight.

Strangely, nothing happened for over an hour. Fargo stayed behind the slab, occasionally peering out or stealthily wending his way to the crest to see if the *vaqueros* on either side were on the move, but they stayed where they were and only fired a few shots, none of which came very close.

Then he heard the approaching riders.

Crouching, he stared in the direction of the plateau and discovered a group of ten or more being led by the *vaquero* who had galloped off earlier. Even at a distance he recognized the big shape of Jesse Walker and Walker's men. As they drew nearer he spied Rojos.

One other person stood out from the rest because she was the only woman. Her long hair flying, riding as well or better than many of her men, Gitana Otero was at the head of the group beside the *vaquero*. She wore a long brown skirt and a brown jacket. A black hat crowned her head.

Fargo was surprised. By all rights Gitana should be at the *hacienda*, not out tracking him down. Why was she taking such a risk? He watched them enter the trees and glimpsed them dismounting and spreading out. The pines were just out of pistol range and he wasn't about to waste a shot until they attacked.

Minutes later a gruff voice bawled out for all to hear: "Fargo! This is Walker! We want to talk!"

"Go to hell!" Fargo responded. He didn't trust Walker as far as he could toss the Ovaro, and he wasn't about to walk down there and get his head blown off.

"We won't shoot," Walker shouted.

Fargo didn't bother to answer. He rested his right hand on the Dragoon and wished Walker would come within range.

"Skye!" Gitana Otero called out. "I'm coming up! And I am unarmed!"

He saw her appear, Rojos and Walker at her side. She spoke to them and they stayed where they were as she boldly crossed to the hill and started upward. Her eyes found him and stayed locked on his until she halted ten feet below the slab and took a deep breath.

Gitana brushed at her hair and smirked. "Is the brave Trailsman afraid to step out and talk with a woman?"

Fargo warily emerged. He doubted Gitana's own men would open fire with her so close, but Walker and company were another matter. "Do we have anything left to talk about?"

"A few things, I think."

"Such as?"

"I'll never forgive you for murdering Reyes," Gitana said bitterly.

"You walked all the way up here to tell me that?"

"No," she said, shaking her head. "Not really."

Fargo waited.

"I want to know why," Gitana said. "Why did you turn against me? I would have honored my promise and paid you in gold for your services. All you had to do was locate the Chiricahua village and tell me where it was." She shook her head in disbelief. "What made you side with the stinking Apaches?"

"I've lived with Indians, remember? They're people, Gitana, not animals. They don't deserve to be sold like cattle and forced to work as slaves."

Gitana uttered a scornful snort. "No one ever told me you were so noble."

"I'm nothing of the kind. I'm just a man trying to live the best I know how."

"You won't be living much longer. We have enough men here to guarantee you won't leave this hill alive."

Fargo gazed at the trees and detected movement, more men moving in both directions to enclose the hill in a ring of firearms. "So I see."

"It was Walker who figured out you might head this way," Gitana boasted. "He said that an Indian lover like you would try to reach the village, so we posted men along the way just in case." She chuckled. "He's not as dumb as he looks."

"You could have fooled me."

Gitana stared at him for a moment. "My father was right about you. That day we arrived, he told me to get rid of you, that you would be trouble. I should have listened to him." She turned and took several strides, then abruptly halted and reached up to remove her hat.

Why would she do that? Fargo wondered, and instantly threw himself to the left, suspecting the action was a signal. His hunch proved correct. Even as he moved a rifle boomed in the trees. He felt a faint breeze fan his right ear and heard a buzzing noise, and then he was behind the slab and safe.

The thought that Gitana had deliberately lured him into the open to give one of her men a clear shot served as a reminder that she was extremely devious. Crouching, he eased to the edge of the rock.

Gitana was in full flight to the base of the hill, her hat still on her head. She glanced over her shoulder in apparent fear of receiving a bullet in the back and nearly tripped. At the bottom she paused to scan the slabs, as if puzzled, and then ran into the trees where Walker and Rojos waited. All three vanished.

Fargo wished he had ammunition for the rifle. He figured the attack would come soon. Jesse Walker didn't impress him as the most patient of men and Walker would likely oversee the rush up the hill.

Staying low, using every available cover, the big man worked his way to the north, away from the slab where they'd last seen him. He angled toward the rim, knowing they would come at him from all sides at once and wanting the best vantage point. A round, four-foot high boulder situated within a yard of the crest afforded the ideal spot to make his stand; he could see both slopes clearly and they would be forced to aim sharply upward at an awkward angle.

No sooner was he in place than a revolver on the west side

fired twice in succession and was promptly answered by a gun to the east. Seconds later men charged from concealment on both sides, those on the west shooting at the slab Fargo had vacated, those on the east simply sprinting all out to reach the top.

Fargo drew the Dragoon and the other revolver. Cocking both hammers, he waited until he had perfect targets on both sides. He raised the Dragoon and shot one of Walker's men coming up the west side, then shifted and used the other gun to shoot a *vaquero* to the east.

Since the lower half of the hill lacked any cover whatsoever, the charging men had no recourse but to drop flat and blast away wildly at the summit.

With lead zinging off boulders all around him, Fargo took deliberate aim and shot another one of Walker's men to the west. The killer was flipped onto his back, then lay still. A bullet thudded into the ground within inches of Fargo's boots and he twisted to see a reckless *vaquero* barreling straight at him up the east side. Extending the heavy '47 Walker Colt, Fargo placed a ball in the center of the man's chest.

The *vaquero* screeched and tumbled.

Gitana's men broke and ran. With four dead in the opening seconds of the fight, they realized they were at too great a disadvantage. They were exposed and vulnerable on the lower slopes and didn't like it one bit.

Fargo could have shot two or three in the back but refrained. He hoped he'd discouraged them enough to prevent them from trying again any time soon. Squatting, he reloaded both weapons and listened to yelling in the trees to the west. It sounded as if Jesse Walker was bawling his men out over their failure.

The big man decided to change position again. Crouching, he scrambled from boulder to tree to boulder until he was at the center of the hill, directly above the slab sheltering the Ovaro. A stunted tree with a thick base became his new vantage point. He settled down on his side, a pistol in each hand, and waited for them to make the next move.

A half hour went by and nothing happened.

Fargo's attention perked up when a rider, staying far out of range, rode in a loop from the west to the east. He saw the man talking to a *vaquero* and figured a message was being relayed from Gitana or Walker. The rider retraced his route, and in a short while there was a lot of activity on both sides. He could see men going around gathering armfuls of dry brush and others tying the collected branches into large bundles that were secured on the ends of their lariats.

The reason was obvious. He lifted his right hand and tested the wind, which turned out to be blowing from the northwest to the southeast, favoring Walker and those to the west. If he was right, they would set the bundles ablaze, wait until smoke poured from each one, then mount their horses and race back and forth along the bottom of his hill until the smoke obscured most of the lower portion. At a prearranged a signal, a shot perhaps, all the men would gallop up the hill with their guns spitting lead. He wouldn't stand a prayer.

Fargo calmly glimpsed the bundles being lit, then crept down until he was behind the slab once more. Sticking the Walker Colt under his belt, he mounted the pinto and moved to the end of the slab.

Soon, hollering and whooping, men began moving along the bottom of the hill, doing as he'd anticipated, trailing smoking bundles in their wake. It didn't take long for the smoke to form a thick cloud and to spread upward.

Holding the reins in one hand, the Dragoon in the other, Fargo scanned the western base of the hill. He could barely distinguished the riders and their animals. Soon they would stop and mount their next attack. He spurred the Ovaro from hiding, moved between the last of the rocks, and headed for the bottom and freedom.

The stallion jerked its head back as its sensitive nostrils inhaled the acrid smoke, but the Ovaro never slowed. Fargo leaned forward as he covered a narrow barren strip and plunged into the cloud. Almost immediately he had to rein up short to avoid colliding with one of Walker's killers who was riding straight at him.

A pistol in hand, the man did a double take at the sight of the Trailsman.

The reaction proved costly. Fargo sent a slug into the rider's brain, then cut to the right and rode hard through the stinging gray cloud until the pinto burst out into fresh air. Behind him arose a jumble of shouts in both English and Spanish. He found himself bearing northwest, well clear of the trees where Gitana and her men had concealed themselves, and kept going.

His strategy had worked. He'd be well clear of the area before they awoke to the trick and came after him. Or so he thought until he glanced around and saw Jose Rojos at the edge of the cloud, pointing at him and roaring madly to get the rest to give chase.

Fargo resigned himself to trying to elude them once more. He gazed ahead at the east slope of the plateau and decided to go all the way to the top. Since he knew of two other ways down, ways they weren't aware of, he might be able to give Gitana and her crew the slip. Not that he would use the western precipice again unless his very life depended on it. But if he could reach the south ridge well ahead of them, he stood a fair chance of finally being rid of his problem.

He stuck to the trail the Apaches had regularly used, covering hundreds of yards before Rojos and twelve or more riders started after him. Riding at the forefront beside the foreman was Gitana Otero.

The Ovaro attained the foot of the east slope and began climbing toward the rim. Fargo looked to his rear at the Otero hands, who were passing between tracks of heavy forest. He suddenly spotted figures moving among the trees a few dozen yards in front of Gitana. With a start he saw they were Apaches.

Fargo reined up and swung the pinto sideways. There were at least eight warriors on each side of the trail, and they were taking aim with bows and arrows, hefting lances, or pointing guns.

Neither Gitana or her men realized the danger they were in. They were all intent on their quarry.

There was nothing the big man could do, even had he wanted to warn them.

Gitana Otero and her *vaqueros* rode directly into the ambush. Arrows cleaved the air, lances streaked from the brush, and a few guns cracked. Six riders and three horses went down in a confused heap amid screaming and shrieking. The rest stopped in confusion, looking every which way, and the Chiricahuas streamed from the forest to fight at close quarters. More arrows sped from powerful bows. In the blink of an eye three *vaqueros* were slain. Those few still alive wheeled their animals and fled in panic, but the warriors weren't about to let them. Two more fell, transfixed through their backs, leaving a single lucky soul to ride frantically to the southeast.

The Apaches began moving among the bodies, finishing off those still breathing, taking scalps and removing everything of possible value.

"It is over."

Fargo turned in surprise at the sound of the voice. Not ten feet away was Chihuahua, astride the black stallion with the Spanish saddle. The chief's features were haggard, his shoulders slumped.

"Maybe now my people can live without fear of being sold as slaves," Chihuahua went on, moving forward until he was beside the Ovaro. He looked at the Trailsman. "Nalin helped me escape from the village yesterday. We hid in the forest and saw those butchers slaughter helpless women and children." He paused. "We also saw you try to help. For that, I thank you."

"Where are the rest of your people?"

"There are caves on the northest side of the plateau. We moved there after the raid. Now we can rebuild our village by the lake, if we want, or anywhere else."

The big man pointed at the warriors milling about the corpses. "Did you set the ambush?"

"I knew Otero's men would be back to try and finish us off so I posted warriors near this trail to keep watch. When they heard shooting earlier, one rode to the caves to let us know. Every man took up his weapons and came here. We had no idea what was happening until we saw you riding toward us with Otero and her killers after you," Chihuahua related. "Nana led our men on foot to avenge the deaths of our loved ones."

Fargo recognized the tall warrior among those stripping clothes off the dead *vaqueros*. "I'm grateful for the help."

"What will you do now? Whcre will you go?"

"Wherever the wind blows me."

Chihuahua smiled and urged his horse down the trail. "I will escort you past our warriors. Some of them might be tempted to put an arrow in you."

Nana and the other Apaches looked up as the weary chief

and the Trailsman approached. Nana came forward waving a scalp in his left hand and grinning in triumph.

Fargo wasn't bothered by the sight; he'd seen more than his share of such grisly trophies. He surveyed the dead and spied Rojos. Two shafts jutted from the foreman's chest. Nearby was one of Walker's men, a lance in his side.

Chihuahua and Nana conversed in their own tongue.

Glancing to the left, Fargo found Gitana Otero. She was on her back between two horses, her face composed as if in sleep. Since Apaches didn't scalp women, her hair was still on her head. The feathered end of an arrow protruding from above her right breast. Her lifeless glassy eyes were open, staring at the azure sky. On an impulse he dismounted, knelt next to her, and gently closed her eyelids.

Some of the Apaches watched him closely, several with hateful expressions.

"You should be on your way," Chihuahua mentioned. "There are friends of Mangus here."

Fargo glanced up and counted five warriors who appeared ready to hurl themselves at him. Chihuahua would be unable to stop them if they did. Most Indian chiefs functioned more as tribal advisers than commanders, and any warrior was free to do as he pleased at any time. He hesitated. Even though Gitana had wound up as his enemy, they'd been on friendly terms once and had shared a night together. He didn't like the notion of leaving her there to rot or of animals feasting on her flesh.

"Why do you delay?" Chihuahua asked.

"I'd like to bury her."

Chihuahua studied him for a moment. "I know of your white custom. But she wanted to kill you, did she not?"

Fargo nodded.

"I see." The chief stared at the lovely corpse. "Very well. You fought the Oteros on our behalf. I will see that a shallow grave is dug."

The big man let his eyes express his gratitude. He swung onto the Ovaro, nodded at Nana, and rode away without a backward glance.

There was no sign of life at the *hacienda* when Fargo rode

into the back yard late in the afternoon. He'd seen plenty of cattle and horses on his way in, but not one *vaquero*. Now, as he reined up a few yards shy of the portico and surveyed the various buildings, he concluded that every last hand must be gone.

Then he heard a loud thump and a tinkling noise from inside the house.

Fargo dismounted, drew the Dragoon, and cautiously walked to the back door. He heard muted voices within. Easing the door open, he glided inside and along the corridor until he came to the kitchen.

Dolorita and three other servants were engrossed in packing Otero possessions into four crates that were almost filled to the brim. All of them jumped at the sound of his voice.

"Where is everyone?"

"Fargo!" Dolorita declared happily, and came over. "You scared us to death. The Apaches are on their way to kill us all."

"Who told you this?"

"One of the *vaqueros*. He raced back over an hour ago and told us Gitana, Rojos, and all the men with them were massacred by the Chiricahuas. He said a huge war party is on its way here."

"And everyone fled," Fargo deduced, sliding the Dragoon into his holster.

"*Si.* We are the last to go. We have a wagon in the front and soon we will load it and leave."

"That's a good idea," Fargo said. He suspected that Nana just might pay the *hacienda* a visit.

"Oh. Before I forget," Dolorita said, "come with me." She brushed past him and led the way to the sitting room. Stopping in the doorway, she pointed at a table in the corner. "I believe those are yours, yes?"

The Sharps, the .44, and the Arkansas toothpick were lying side by side.

Fargo eagerly went over to reclaim his weapons. He placed the Dragoon and the Walker Colt on the table.

"One of the men wanted to take them but I stopped him," Dolorita said as he was sliding the throwing knife into his boot, "I told him that you might still be alive and he would not want to have you on his trail."

159

"Thanks."

She cocked her head. "Were you there? Did you see it?"

Fargo nodded. He began reloading the .44.

"Did she suffer?"

"No."

Dolorita sighed. "That is good." She turned and hastened off. "I must finish packing, *senor*."

He finished reloading, then took the Sharps out to the Ovaro. After leaning the other rifle against the porch, he slid the Sharps into the holster and stood back. Now he could leave.

A horse whinnied in the stable.

Fargo shifted to thoughtfully regard the building. There were horses still inside, locked in their stalls. Without anyone to feed them, they might well starve before anyone came to investigate the stories the hands were bound to tell to authorities both north and south of the border. The animals should be released so they could forage for themselves.

He strolled into the stable and walked down the aisle. The body of Reyes Feliz had been removed. Four horses were in stalls on the right-hand side and he promptly set about letting them go. He had to shoo two of them before they would trot outside.

At the entrance he paused to scan the estate, and it was then that a shot boomed from somewhere to the south and a slug slammed into the wall within inches of his head. The Colt leaped clear and he darted back from view.

"Didn't think I'd let you get away that easily, did you?" yelled a gruff voice.

Fargo knew who was out there: Jessie Walker. The hardcase's body had been conspicuously absent from those at the scene of the slaughter, and on the way back from the mountains Skye had speculated on where the killer might be. Had Walker possessed a shred of common sense, he would have headed out of the territory as fast as his mount could carry him.

"Show yourself, you son of a bitch!"

He guessed that Walker was behind one of the trees in the yard, covering the stable with a rifle. Checking the aisle to his rear he discovered a pitchfork leaning against a stall. Just what he needed. He brought it to the doorway clasped in his left hand, then tensed and tossed the implement to the left as far as he could.

A shot rang out and a bullet struck the pitchfork in the handle.

Fargo was in motion the very instant he released the fork. He was out of the stable and sprinting to the right as the shot thundered, and he glimpsed gun smoke and a figure standing at the corner of the house. By the time the shooter realized he'd been tricked, Fargo was at a tree and flush with the trunk. He peeked out to find the figure had vanished.

Crouching, Fargo dashed toward the same corner, ready to squeeze off a shot, but Walker had fled. He leaned against the wall and heard a hard crash out front punctuated by a scream.

Dolorita!

Fargo sprinted to the next corner and carefully took a look. A male servant was sprawled unconscious on the front steps. Standing in the bed of the wagon was another man and a woman. He ran toward them, prudently ducking under each window he passed, until he stood near the wide open front door. "Dolorita?"

The man in the wagon gulped and pointed at the doorway.

He understood. Frowning, he inched closer to peek past the jamb. Midway down the hall stood Dolorita, frightened out of her wits, and standing behind her, his revolver pressed to her head, was Jesse Walker.

The regulator grinned. "About time you showed up. Throw your gun down and step in here where I can get a good look at you."

Fargo wasn't about to do any such thing. He debated trying to shoot Walker but didn't have a clear enough shot.

"I won't wait all day, scum," Walker snapped. "Feliz told me about you and this filly here. So either you step out in the open like I told you, or she gets a bullet in the brain. Which will it be?"

Skye withdrew a few steps and glanced at his Colt. He couldn't let Dolorita be killed, but he didn't want to commit suicide, either. Did Walker know he had found his own weapons? Probably not. If so, he had a slim chance. Leaning down, he removed the throwing knife and cupped the hilt in his left palm, then stepped to the edge of the doorway and gazed at Walker and the maid.

"I'll count to three," Walker taunted.

"There's no need," Fargo said. He bent at the knees and slid the .44 along the floor for over a yard. Straightening, keeping his arms out of sight, he transferred the knife to his right hand and held it so that the weapon was hidden by his forearm.

Jesse Walker chortled. "I didn't really think you'd do it," he said.

"Let the woman go."

"Not until you step into the hall."

Taking a deep breath, Fargo did just that, his arms hanging at his sides.

"You're a jackass, Fargo," Walker declared, and gave Dolorita a shove that drove her to her knees. "I wouldn't give my life for anyone."

"That's the difference between you and me," Fargo said, walking forward. He needed to reduce the distance by half to guarantee an accurate throw. If he could only keep the hardcase talking long enough.

"You have more lives than a cat," Walker said, "but here is where your string of luck runs out. You cost me five good men, damn your hide." He took a step and pointed his weapon.

"Go ahead and fire," Fargo said, still advancing slowly.

Walker blinked, then wagged his revolver. "You want me to shoot?"

"Sure. It will make it that much easier for the Apaches to find you. They should be here about now."

"The Apaches?"

"They were about ten minutes behind me when I left the foothills," Fargo bluffed.

Walker's brow knit and he started to turn his head, then thought better of the idea. "You're lying," he declared, steadying his gun.

Fargo paused. He had six or seven feet to cover before he would be close enough to suit him. "You know damn well the Apaches won't be satisfied with killing the Oteros." He took another step. "They'll want to burn this place to the ground."

And another. "Where did you leave your horse, anyway? Think you can reach it before the Chiricahuas get here?"

The strain of deep concentration showed on Walker's brow. He was a brutal man accustomed to a hard life of violent action, not a deep thinker. But in his own way, where killing was concerned, he could be as devious as a sly fox. So it took him several seconds to realize the Trailsman was trying to trick him. Once he did, he smirked, aimed, and took a stride, his finger tightening on the trigger.

Fargo had nowhere to go, nowhere to take shelter. He saw the barrel point at his chest and braced for the impact when the unforeseen transpired. In Walker's eagerness to shoot him, the hardcase forgot about Dolorita, who had not budged since falling to her knees. Walker inadvertently bumped into her and nearly fell, throwing his aim off, his shot plowing into the wall on Fargo's left. Dolorita screamed in sheer terror.

The double distraction was all the opening Fargo needed. Walker's eyes flicked down at the woman and in that instant Fargo took a bound and whipped his right arm in an overhand arc, the glittering blade flying from his hand as Walker straightened. The knife sped true, the keen tip slicing into Walker's neck, the blade burying itself all the way.

About to shoot again, Walker went rigid in shock, then dropped his revolver and desperately clawed at the knife. He staggered backward, wheezing, blood seeping from the corners of his mouth. Suddenly unable to stand, he sank to his knees and gurgled.

Fargo ran to Dolorita and picked up Walker's gun. He impassively stood and watched the man die, watched as Walker jabbed a finger at him and tried to utter a curse, watched as Walker sputtered and finally pitched onto his face with a sickening splat.

He leaned down and helped the maid to rise. "Snap out of it," he said. "You must get in that wagon and leave. Now."

Dolorita nodded absently. She glanced at the hardcase and shuddered. "Thank you. I thought he would kill me."

"The Apaches just might if you don't get going," Fargo said. "I'll get my horse and ride with you a ways."

She moved unsteadily toward the door, gaining strength with every step.

Fargo recovered his .44 and went outside. The unconscious servant was just being revived. He handed Walker's weapon to the other man and hastened around back where the Ovaro stood munching on grass. Once mounted, he escorted the wagon eastward until they came to the narrow track that led southward toward Mexico.

Dolorita, seated beside the driver, gazed fondly at him and smiled. "I thank you for everything."

"It's a long ride to Mexico by wagon," Fargo pointed out. "Can you get there in one piece?"

"We will do fine. Don Otero brought us up this way, remember? The trail is well marked and we have several guns."

"Be careful," Fargo said.

"We will." Dolorita held out her hand. "I'll never forget you."

The big man gave her fingers a squeeze, then stayed at the junction as the wagon lumbered ponderously southward. Once it was out of sight he turned the pinto toward the eastern pass. The sun was low on the horizon when he reached the trail that wound up from the valley floor. Pausing, he gazed toward the *hacienda* and heard faint war whoops.

By the time Sky Fargo reached the rim of the pass, huge clouds of black smoke billowed from the grand house and the outbuildings while bright tongues of red and orange flames licked at the walls. He faced westward for a minute, witnessing the end of a ranching dynasty that stretched back centuries, a dynasty built on pure greed. Then he shrugged and rode into the wilderness to meet his future.

LOOKING FORWARD!

**The following is the opening
section from the next novel in the exciting
Trailsman series from Signet:**

THE TRAILSMAN #119
RENEGADE RIFLES

*1860, just south of the Salt Fork Red,
in the land the government called
the Indian Territory but the settlers
called hell's empire . . . .*

His first glimpse of the young woman was a figure sliding down an embankment. She landed at the bottom and he waited to see if a horse followed her. But nothing else slid down the steep side of the embankment and he watched the young woman pick herself up and begin to run toward a thick stand of blackjack oak.

She ran with terror in her every movement, legs driving, arms held stiffly, casting quick glances behind her. Tall, with dusty-blond hair flowing out behind her, a torn brown dress allowed glimpses of strong, shapely legs. The big man's lake-blue eyes narrowed as he watched her disappear into the oak. She was plainly running from something and he sat unmoving in the saddle. The stand of oak was narrow. She'd be at the other end in minutes. He moved forward a few paces but stayed inside the cluster of box elder.

He had spent the day riding leisurely northward, up from Quanah, letting the magnificent Ovaro set its own pace, the animal's jet-black fore and hindquarters and pure white midsection glistening in the hot sun. Now he moved another few paces inside the trees and the young woman flashed into sight. She paused to catch her breath and glanced fearfully right and left before turning to run toward a larger and thicker stand of oak. Then suddenly he saw why she fled as the three small but sturdy Indian ponies appeared atop a low rise of land, each carrying a bare-chested rider. The three bucks halted, their eyes sweeping the terrain. It took only a moment for them to find their quarry as the sunlight caught the dusty-blond hair in a yellow flash against the dark green foliage.

Skye Fargo leaned forward in the saddle as the young woman saw the three figures start to move after her along the top of the rise. She tried to run faster and only succeeded in stumbling and falling forward. She picked herself up at once and continued for the stand of oaks. But the fall had cost her almost a half-minute and the three Indians were halfway down the slope now. Fargo's eyes went to the oaks and back to the girl. She'd never reach the trees in time, he was certain. He spurred the Ovaro forward toward the fleeing girl. But he stayed in the trees that stretched out before him until they joined the main stand of oaks. The treeline curved and took him a dozen yards from the fleeing figures. He had to stay inside the cover and a quick glance backward showed him the three bucks were on the level ground now, their ponies going full out.

Fargo's hand reached down to the big Colt at his side but he quickly let the gun drop back into its holster. The three bucks might not be alone. Shots would surely bring any others nearby. He kept the pinto running through the trees as his eyes watched the three Indians that were almost abreast of him, now. Each carried a rifle, he saw, one a new Henry and the other two Smith & Wesson Volcanics. His eyes switched to the young woman. She was nearing the oaks but she was running out of time, the three bucks closing in fast now. Fargo brought his concentration back to skirting tree trunks as he put the Ovaro into a gallop and he reached the place where his tree cover joined the heavy stand of oak. He raced into the oak, slowed and saw that the three horsemen had reached the fleeing young woman, not more than a dozen yards from where he was inside the trees.

One bent low from the back of his pony, reached out and

grabbed a handful of dusty-blond hair. The young woman screamed in pain as he yanked her back and flung her to the ground. The other two were already off their ponies and seized her at once. One, a narrow-framed buck with his thick, black hair in two braids, pulled the girl to her feet, a grin of anticipation on his face. The third buck had dismounted and stepped up to pull the young woman's head up and backward. She was good-looking, Fargo noted, high-cheekboned with a small nose and a face that had strength even in pain and fright.

Fargo reined to a halt inside the oak stand, the trio holding the girl directly in front of him. His eyes swept the scene, taking in every detail of the three Indians with the precise absorption that was an automatic thing, as much a part of him as breathing. He felt a furrow dig into his brow for a moment as he dropped to the ground on the balls of his feet with the silence of a mountain cat. He knelt, reached down and drew the knife from the narrow leather holster he wore around his calf. He turned the blade in his hand, a perfectly balanced throwing knife, thin and double-edged with each edge razor sharp, the kind often called an Arkansas toothpick.

He moved forward, to the very edge of the trees as two of the bucks threw the young woman on the ground. She kicked out with both legs and again he saw long, lovely limbs. The third brave fell atop her, pressing her legs apart as the other two held her arms stretched upward. The buck wore loose cotton leggings of the kind favored by the Apache and he had the front open in seconds. He reached up to tear the young woman's underclothes away. He was laughing and his companions joined in with deep, grunting sounds, a kind of obscene cheerleading. Fargo chose the one holding the girl's right arm, took another half-second to aim and sent the blade hurtling through the air with all the power of his arm and shoulder muscles.

He watched the blade slam into the center of the man's chest and bury itself up to the hilt. The Indian dropped his hands from the young woman's arm as he staggered backward. Surprise flooded his face first, utter and total surprise as he looked down at the knife hilt in his chest. The pain came next as his mouth fell open and his eyes grew wide. He staggered back another two steps, tried to pull the blade from his chest but the hand that closed around the hilt of the knife had already lost its strength. Slowly, with a half-spiral, he sank to the ground and lay still.

Fargo's eyes went to the other two bucks. Both had let go of the young woman and were frozen in a half-crouch, rifles raised, peering forward into the trees. A sudden and complete silence had descended on the scene. Even the young woman froze in place as she lay propped up on her elbows on the ground. The two braves were listening, straining their ears, Fargo realized. He remained equally silent and motionless, a thin smile on his face. He saw one of them flick his hand, a quick leftward motion and the other one immediately darted away in a crouch. He ran for the trees while the first one ran to the other side.

Both moved into the oaks, one to his left, one to his right and Fargo glanced at the young woman again. She was sitting up but she watched the two Indians move into the trees. Surprise and fear held her frozen and he returned his attention to the trees. The two bucks stayed silent and unmoving for a full two minutes. Fargo stayed equally silent in the high brush, hardly breathing. The two braves started to move, a dozen darting steps and then a pause to listen again, waiting to pick up a telltale sound, the movement of brush, the soft sound of dirt being scraped by a footstep. Fargo's smile was thin. This time their quarry could think as well as react by instinct.

He chose the brave to his right, gathered his muscles and was ready when the Indian moved again. Fargo moved at the same time. When the Indian halted, he halted, too. The buck moved again and Fargo moved with him, using the Indian's movements as cover for his own. Once again the buck halted to listen and once again he heard nothing. But he was close, now, and Fargo could see him through the foliage. The other one was still a fair distance away. The Indian moved again, another dozen quick steps, and then dropped to one knee to listen for the sound of his quarry. But again Fargo had moved with him. He was almost directly behind the Indian now. He knew he'd have but one chance to strike and make the strike swift and noiseless.

He rose up on the balls of his feet, not unlike a runner at the starting line. The buck was in front of him, listening as he peered through the trees. He had the rifle in one hand, held near to his side. Fargo dove forward in one motion as fluid as water leaving the neck of a jar. The buck caught the movement of air behind him, started to spin but Fargo was on him, one hand closing around the rifle at the breech. He brought the gun upward, closed his other hand around the end of the barrel and jammed the gun horizontally against the buck's throat as he pulled backward. The Indian fell against him as Fargo pulled against the rifle again and felt the man's throat collapse inward.

The buck slid down to the ground as Fargo pulled the rifle from his throat. It had taken not more than a half-dozen seconds and it had been almost noiseless, just the rustle of brush and the tiny gasped choke. But almost wasn't good enough. The other buck had heard and Fargo heard him charging. The Trailsman spun as the Indian raised the rifle and fired, still charging, the shot too hasty, the bullet too high. Fargo dipped as he brought up a left hook in a blazing arc. The Indian was still charging as the blow smashed into his jaw and Fargo heard the sound of bone cracking.

The buck stopped as though he had run into a stone wall. The rifle dropped from his hand and Fargo caught it before it hit the ground. He smashed the heavy stock across the man's head as the Indian was already collapsing. The blow ensured he'd not get up again. Fargo spun away with a silent curse on his lips. The Indian had gotten off one shot and that could be more than enough. He ran from the trees to see the young woman on her feet and starting to flee. She halted when he called out. She turned and saw him and a wave of relief flooded her face.

She was more attractive than he'd been able to see—full lips, a tall frame with full breasts and hazel eyes that held a direct, strong gaze. She ran toward him and he caught her by the arm. "Into the trees. That shot could bring more," he said.

"No, those three were the only ones chasing me," she said. "The others are half a mile away, attacking the wagons. I was running to find help." Fargo gave a low whistle and the Ovaro trotted from the trees. "You've got to go back with me and help those poor people in the wagons," the young woman said. He nodded but paused to kneel down beside the first buck and pull his knife free, his eyes sweeping the prostrate form of the Indian as he cleaned the blade on the grass. Once again, he felt the furrow cross his brow but he rose, swung onto the Ovaro and pulled the young woman up behind him in the saddle.

Her arms went around his waist and he felt the warmth of her against his back. She smelled of perspiration and powder, a musky dark odor that was strangely attractive. "Which way?" he asked.

"North, over the ridge and across the next hill," she said.

"How'd you get away?" he asked as he put the pinto into a gallop and felt her breasts bouncing against him.

"We had stopped. I'd gone off to pick berries when they attacked. I hid at first, and then tried to run. But those three saw me and came after me. Maybe if I'd had a horse I could've gotten away from them."

"Just the opposite," Fargo said. "You managed to avoid being caught for as long as you did because you were on foot. They'd have caught you real quick if you'd been on horseback."

"You might be right. I was able to go into every little crevice and gully. I thought I'd gotten away from them at one point but then they spotted me again," she said. Fargo fell silent, concentrated on riding hard and felt her arms grow tighter around his waist. He kept the Ovaro at a gallop as he climbed the ridge, then the hill and slowed as he neared the crest. A quick glance skyward showed him that there weren't more than two hours of daylight left. He heard the wild whoops, unmistakable and always chilling, as he crested the hill. An expanse of post oak swept down the hill to let him keep racing forward until he drew closer to the bottom.

He saw the wagons then, three of them, halted against a line of cottonwoods. He halted beneath one of the oaks and slid from the saddle, the girl coming with him. He dropped to one knee as his gaze swept the scene. Some two dozen bucks, he counted, exuberantly racing back and forth alongside the wagons. The attack was over, a half-dozen bodies hanging over the sides of the three Conestogas. "What are you stopping here for?" he heard the young woman ask. "We've got to go down and help them."

"It's too late," Fargo said grimly.

"You don't know that."

"I know it," he said.

"We can't just sit here and watch. Shoot some of them. Chase them away. Do something, damn you," she said and he saw her face was white with strain, her hands clenched into fists.

"That'd be committing suicide, nothing more," he said.

"Why'd you come then if you weren't going to help?" she flung at him, fury in her hazel eyes.

"I hoped I could help. I might have, if the fight was still going on. But not now. It's too late," he said.

"It's not too late for me," she snapped and spun on her heel, yanked the rifle from the saddle holster of the Ovaro and started to bring the gun around. She was upset beyond reason, caught up in the kind of fury and anguish that snaps the mind. He leaped, twisted the rifle from her hands and his blow just grazed the tip of her pretty chin. But it was enough and he saw her eyes flutter shut as she started to go down. He caught her with one arm and lowered her gently to the ground.

Jamming the rifle back into its holster, he returned to one knee and watched the scene at the now silent wagons. The furrow that had touched his brow earlier returned but now as a full-fledged frown. The braves had dismounted and three tore the canvas top from the lead Conestoga, then ripped the arched bows away to allow more room inside the wagon. Fargo's frown deepened as he saw other braves carry lamps, small dressers, pots and pans, a bedstand table plus the headboard and footboard of a bed, another larger dresser and finally a sewing machine, from the other two wagons and load everything into the first.

While he watched in consternation, one brave took the reins of the Conestoga and began to drive the wagon upward along a shallow rise while the others rode their ponies alongside. He was watching them move away when a small groan broke into his thoughts and he turned to see the young woman stir, pull her eyes open and sit up. She stared at him for a moment and her slap grazed the side of his cheek just as he managed to pull back in time. "Bastard. Coward," she hissed.

He caught her wrist and yanked her around hard so she could see the last of the Indians disappear into the trees. "It's done, finished, dammit," he hissed. "No more out of you." She glared at him as he let her wrist go. "Damnedest thing I've ever seen. I'm thinking about following them," he said. "There's only a half hour of daylight left."

"There could be people still alive in the wagons," she said.

"Alive enough to get to town and a doctor. That's more important than chasing after those savages."

"Red Sand's the nearest town. That's a good ten miles north into Oklahoma Territory," he said.

"That's where we were going," she said. He drew a deep sigh and met her pain-filled anger with a grimace. There was a glimmer of truth in her words. There was always the chance that life still flickered. He rose, pulled her to her feet and began to walk down the hill toward the wagons, the Ovaro following behind. She caught up with him to walk beside him. The furrow was still digging into his brow when he reached the remaining two wagons and he cast a quick glance at the young woman. She had steeled herself for what they saw, jaw tight, shoulders thrown back and her full breasts straining the top of the brown dress. She had her own determined strength, he saw; no flinching in her as they halted beside the arrow-riddled bodies.

He had seen worse. There'd been no time for mutilation and there were only three scalpings. He walked slowly among the bodies littering the ground and pulled the canvas back on each wagon to look at those still inside. The young woman stayed with him and he heard her quick, sharp gasps of breath. Finally he halted and turned to her. None were clinging to life. "There were three children, two boys and a girl," she said. "They're not here. You think they got away?"

He shook his head. "How old were they?"

"Nine to eleven," she said.

"They were taken off before we got here," he said.

"Oh, God," she breathed. "I've heard that happens."

"It does. It's the only thing about this that fits," he said as she frowned.

"Meaning what?" she asked.

"I don't know what," Fargo said as dusk began to roll across the dip of the land. "I'll take you to Red Sand."

"You sure it won't inconvenience you," she said, an edge of disdain suddenly in her voice.

"Watch your damn tongue, honey," Fargo said. "Or I might just leave you to walk."

"That wouldn't surprise me," she sniffed and he fastened her with a glare.

"You still stewing because I wouldn't rush in shooting like a damn fool?" he questioned.

"Yes. Maybe it'd have saved one life," she snapped.

"It'd have ended mine," he said. "And yours." She glared back, refusing to concede. "You can think whatever the hell you like about me, honey. I don't give a damn." He spun from her and pulled himself onto the Ovaro.

"No, I don't suppose you do," she said.

"I saved your ass and your scalp," he said. "You can remember that while you're walking." He turned the Ovaro, flicked the reins and the horse started off.

"Wait," he heard the young woman call out and he reined to a halt. She hurried up to him. "You did," she said, the anger out of her face. "Maybe I've been too harsh."

"Maybe?" he echoed.

Her lips tightened. "All right, no maybe. I was too harsh."

"Try adding stupid," he said, waited, his face set.

Her eyes flashed. "You enjoy humiliating someone?" she said.

"I enjoy the truth," he said coldly.

She drew a deep breath, her breasts rising beautifully. "All right. I was harsh and stupid. You feel better now?" she asked.

"No, but you should," he answered and she stared back for a long moment.

"Nobody's ever talked that way to me before," she said slowly.

"Too bad," he grunted and reached his hand out. She closed her fingers around his and he pulled her into the saddle, in front of him, this time. The darkness descended as he rode from the dip in the land and the furrow on his brow had returned. It had nothing to do with the young woman leaning back against him. But maybe she knew more than she realized. He'd try to find out on the way to Red Sand.